For Patrice

My Mom the Mouse

A Family Memoir of Questionable Accuracy

BRIAN WEILERT

TIBETAN TREEFROG PUBLISHING

BRIAN WEILERT

TIBETAN TREEFROG PUBLISHING
819 190th Street
Fort Scott, KS 66701

ISBN: **1490909125**
ISBN-13: **978-1490909127**

DEDICATION

This book is dedicated not only to my mom, but to all mothers who work so hard to keep their families glued together.

CONTENTS

BRIAN WEILERT

ACKNOWLEDGMENTS

I want to thank: My son, Baker who said I had to finish a book before he graduated from college, my son Levi for his inspiration through his writing, my co-workers and students at Fort Scott who suffered through early drafts and both encouraged me and edited, and to my family for allowing me the leeway to tell this story as I remembered it. Most of all, I want to thank my loving wife who is always in my corner.

Thieves and Forks

I have a bad habit of getting things stuck in my head late in the evening and I don't mean sharp objects such as number #2 pencils and ice picks, but rather *thoughts* of varying degrees of importance. And by late, I mean the wee hours of the morning. It is always the same.

I will somehow manage to fall asleep, but the slightest of noises: Like our tomcat, Leon the outdoor mouser who accidently gets locked inside tearing at the recliner in the living room because I'm not there to stop him…once a fine piece of furniture now looks as if it should be on a front porch or in the alley with a cardboard sign, *free if you haul*. Slight noises, like that random drip in the wall, hidden behind the sheetrock, that comes and goes for no reason even though I swear to God no water pipes are anywhere near the spot in which I hear it; *I should probably really look into that...black mold and all.* Or, the not-so-slight noise of the coon dogs across the bay whose barks float effortlessly over the water so intensely, I expect to feel the moist slap of their tongues on my forehead...or my wife, Stacia, farting, or me farting, or my too old, too fat dog, Zeke, farting though to be honest it's usually the smell that jars me to consciousness. He sleeps just a few feet from my head, sprawled out on the floor atop my discarded, dirty clothes from the previous day. Apparently, we have varying opinions on the quality of each other's smells...but like I said; the slightest of noises will wake me. I fancy myself a light sleeper; one who is always on guard to protect his family...though my wife would tell a different story.

Heaven help any thieves who might randomly select my home to increase their wealth. Next to Zeke, just under my bed is my 12-gauge. It may be strange, but on many of those sleepless nights I mentally construct a heroic, gun-play script of foiling a would-be intruder.

It goes something like this: I hear the sound of footsteps, wood creaking in the living room and I slide the weapon of mass destruction from its case. My children, now grown, no longer live at home, so a shell is already in place. Don't want the sound of putting one in the chamber to spook him...yes *him*...not being sexist, but it just seems less impressive if the intruder is female, of course I realize this in and of itself makes me sexist. I move from the bed, sliding like a burnt, cheese omelet from one of those infomercial Teflon skillets...smooth...no sound. I avoid the dog. He might be a pain-in-the-ass 90% of the time, but he's the only dog I've ever owned and, though he is nearing that time when I will have to make the cruel decision on the quality of his life versus longevity, I just can't bear the thought of him being shot.

If it goes well, my wife will never know it happened until she is startled into the here-and-now by either the sound of my booming voice or the booming of a gunshot speaking on my behalf; though I have reservations about this. Maybe, I should give her a head's-up... allow her time to slip to the floor on the opposite side of the bed just in case everything plays out wrong? But, I just can't risk her bitching at me, out loud, for waking her up...I would lose my advantage. Besides, what could go wrong when confronting an armed, hardened criminal in the confines of one's home?

I take the time to pull on my slippers, giant monstrosities shaped like Hobbit feet, complete with toe nails and toe hair. They were a gift from my wife last Christmas. They look ridiculous and cool. It takes time, but it is worth it. I now understand how Mr. Baggins could move undetected in the woods. The massive surface area allows me to sneak about the house in complete silence. A tactic I used just the day before to move into position to goose my wife's crotch; a Neanderthal display of affection my father used to gross us kids out with on many occasions. It ranked up there with the boob-grab and the long kiss. I learned how to show my love for my wife by watching my parents. My wife came from a family where there was a *Cleaveresk* peck on the lips before and after work. So, there was a breaking in period. And from her reaction to the most recent goosing...I would argue I still have ground to cover.

I move to the door of my room. Here's the tricky part...I
hear him pattering about, the tinkle of fine china, which we,
of course, don't own...not sure there is any value in fine
china anymore. To be honest, I'm not even sure I know
what it is. I've watched many episodes of Antique
Roadshow, and not once have I witnessed an "OH MY
GOODNESS," moment involving dishes. But, in all
fairness, I don't watch it religiously.

Now, what to do...choice one is to yell from behind the
door, "I have a shotgun and I'm giving you five seconds to
leave my house before I shoot you in half! One, two..." I
feel the graphic nature of *in half* will surely make him
quickly exit if he is at all a visual learner. I would wait a
few more seconds, maybe a minute; listening intently...I
would pinch my nose and blow out to pop my eardrums, a
trick I was taught by my mother when I was younger to
help relieve the pressure from my persistent ear aches.

I had terrible problems growing up. To remedy the
problem, though I am sure this is no longer a preferred
practice, Mom took me to the doctor and held me down
while he punctured each ear drum with a long instrument
that looked very much like a sharpened knitting needle. In
fact, it might have been just that. To this day I remember
the pain. I am also not sure I ever fully forgave my mother
for being the accomplice. But, if I didn't forgive her, it was
tucked away snug in my subconscious...those repressed
memories are harmless...right? When I did this odd ritual
of pinch-n-pop, I felt as if I gained super hearing. Right
after the *pop*, I used to make the Million Dollar Man sound
effect when I was young...*do do do do*...okay, I still might
make the sound. I should mention it is also a helpful

gimmick to equalize pressure when diving in deep water or taking off and landing in a plane.

I would yell one more time, "I am coming out!" which is really stupid. I might as well yell, "Hey, you have been very quiet and to reward your patience and bravery for not fleeing, I am going to give you, first-shot!" Nonetheless, I emerge and he of course is gone, and all is safe. In this scenario, I do not think on what my wife and dog would be doing as it would just complicate the story-line.

Choice #2: I open the door slowly, with no verbal warning issued. The door is going to make sound; even a Hobbit can't prevent this from happening. It might make sense to open it quickly, but I don't. There seems to be a franticness about it that destroys the calm persona I have created for my main character.

On a side note, I sleep naked. I am not the physical specimen I once was…so, for the sake of not being distracted by the many thoughts about the flaws of my nearly fifty year old body; for this scene I have on pajamas. It's weird that I have become so self-conscious as to worry about what the intruder might think. Despite the fact I may indeed shoot him *in half*, the knowledge of him thinking my penis is inadequate with his last thought, is too much. Thus, I am wearing pajamas.

Even though the door makes noise as I peak around the corner, I am in luck as he is distracted looking for the good silver. Again, much like the fine china, I am aware it is an archaic symbol of something valuable in the home. But, there he stands, head down, drawer open…I can hear the cutleries cry out as they bump together. He is digging as if he were me…*looking for that damn lighter I know I put in there the last time the electricity went out!* What he would find in our house, in our drawer, would be an assortment of mismatched spoons, knives and forks; an embarrassment for my wife whenever we have company. But, it just seems silly to buy more when we have so many. It's not like a spoon goes bad…or runs away with the dish.

One particular fork is off to the side, not in the plastic concave mold in the shape of a fork. It mingles amongst the other one-of-a-kind, nomad rebels…roaming free: the potato peeler, the pizza cutter and candy thermometer. The *fork* was relegated as an outcast due to the fact that it is an extension fork; which is to say it was a normal tined utensil combined with a handle made of an old-style TV antenna. It looks normal, but like a super hero, it could stretch to great lengths to snatch a tater-tot from a plate on the other side of the dinner table. Not that this is something a superhero would do; hard to maintain the type of abs that are complimented by spandex whilst consuming greasy carbs.

The *fork* was a novelty purchased for me by my mother about a year before her death. I'm sure she stumbled on to it while browsing in one of those Ozark truck stops. The ones that sell hand carved backscratchers and hillbilly scenes constructed entirely from the husks of walnuts. Not a random gift though, but a purposeful one, meant to both poke fun and share a memory from my childhood.

I was a chubby kid and was always in the kitchen enjoying the company of my mother when she cooked. Now, this is a chicken-egg scenario of where I am not sure if my love of food made me hang around the kitchen, where I spent many wonderful hours with Mom, or because of my love of Mom, I hung out with food…either way I was *pudgy*.

The habit I embraced during my time in the kitchen brings to light this fork tangent; the habit of *picking*. My portly little phalanges were always pulling meat from the roast yet to be served…raw potatoes before their hot bath…fingers cloaked in gravy, soup, frosting licked clean… It drove my mother nuts. She developed a mantra, "Brian, don't pick!" It was half-hearted and really, I couldn't help myself. My mom was sort of to blame. She, a lover of food as well, shared the same portly passion, but as the official cook, it was okay for her as she tasted to see if it was *seasoned right*; though this never explained the raw potatoes which she would salt and pepper before plopping them in her mouth.

But, to the fork…after years of only vocalizing her protest, she took a physical stand one evening. Just as Mom was serving supper, I reached over and grabbed a radish from a veggie tray…which really paints the wrong picture as a *veggie tray* in our house was seven to thirteen radishes cold-water soaking in soup bowl.

I am sure without thinking, and maybe just as an intimidation gesture, Mom jabbed at my hand with a fork she was holding. But, like a warning shot that pierces a man's heart, the fork struck its intended target. The inch-deep blow landed just behind the knuckle of my index finger and stuck like an Oklahoma land-rush, pioneer woman claiming her plot of territory. As I pulled back, the head stayed buried as if it were a stubborn tick; the fork's handle flopping side-to-side in a motion imitating a cat's tail when pissed. I was actually too stunned to say anything…I don't remember it hurting. My mother instantly started to repeat that she was, "Sorry…so sorry." I should note there is a discrepancy in the story that morphed over the years. My mom's interpretation, as I grew to adulthood, was; she *meant* to do it and she was, "Not sorry," as it was, "Well deserved."

Even as I write this, I can look down, some forty years later, and make out two faint scars which look as though I was bitten by the front teeth of a micro-bunny.

This was not Mom and I's first kitchen altercation. I should point out this next story, chronologically out of order, takes place when I was just three, so it is entirely the memory of my mother; an ass-whooping saga passed down orally through the generations. I was a horribly stubborn kid, so the story goes, and my mother had just mopped the linoleum in the kitchen. She looked right at me and stated to stay off the floor until it dried. Again, her story, so I would not be surprised if what actually happened was she whispered it under her breath while looking the opposite direction or said nothing at all.

Within a split second, I had stepped my foot, housed in a muddy, *Ked* tennis shoe, onto the wet floor as if I were playing a game of hokey pokey with a madwoman. For the very moment I *put my right foot in*, she swatted my butt and yelled, "Do not do that again!" I took no notice and the incident repeated itself with a harder swat. Verbal warning...step...harder swat...verbal warning...step...harder swat, swat, swat, swat, swat. My mother admitted this crazed cycle continued until she had to stop due to shame. She said she had beaten my bottom so many times and so hard, the raspberry-raised welts strewn down my tiny thighs cause her great guilt. I intentionally used the word *tiny* when describing my thighs as an attempt to conjure up further pity.

The guilt-trip is a prized skill wielded by every mother worth her salt...I wanted Mom to know she had taught me well. At three, I had won my first battle of *wills*. We would have many more, Mom and I, over the following years with both claiming victories and lamenting defeats.

So, there the intruder stands, rummaging through the silverware unaware of my presence. I lift the gun calmly and say, "Mister, I have a gun pointed right at you and if you move, I am going to shoot you in half." Now, here the story can veer off in two directions. The first is he simply complies. I tell him to lie down and weave his fingers together behind his head...a technique I was taught during my time as a boarding officer in the Coast Guard, and he complies. I tell him if he moves a muscle I will kill him...he doesn't. The rest is pretty boring; call cops, article in the paper...not even worth thinking on and, next to the first option of *him running off without me ever seeing him*, probably the way I would like it to go down in the real world.

The final option, though the best movie material, is not what I want. It does rank highest on the hero scale, but killing a bad-guy is probably not as nifty as everyone envisions it to be. It plays out, roughly, this way…He hears my threat and pulls out a pistol. I react with the reflexes of a skittish kitten and get a shot off before he can even level the gun. He falls to the floor…in half…dead. There is no blood as that is not something you want to think about lying in bed next to your wife late at night. After all, there *really* isn't anyone in the house but the two of us…and Zeke.

Anyway, you get the general idea of my destinationless, mental-wanderings in the middle of the night.

2

The First Encounter

My first glance at the mouse was four years after my
mother's death. I cannot tell you if it was any sort of tragic
anniversary as I do not know the date of her passing. It
may seem insensitive, but I don't want to know...don't
want to remember. Why would I dwell on the worst time I
can remember having in regards to my mother? My wife,
who is Greek, has an opposite take when it comes to death.
She can dig out old, family pictures; faded black and whites
of corpses. Yes, corpses; dressed in their Sunday best,
resting in coffins. I told her it was just morbid; to keep
pictures such as these...like trading cards Jeffery Dahmer
might have collected. Not sure she ever gave me a good
answer as to why these photos were important, but upon
her mother's death, as if a rite of passage, she took her
camera into the funeral parlor and did her daughterly duty.

It was 2:00 am and another sleepless night. I tried to get out of bed quietly, but popping knees and elbows threatened to wake my wife…the self-proclaimed, lightest sleeper…ever! She did not wake. I often told her, she indeed is not a light sleeper and one of these nights I was going to put a pillow over her head and suffocate her to prove it. I told her not to worry as I am sure she would *sleep* through the whole ordeal. She just laughed and asked if I knew how many times over the past twenty five years of marriage she had already done that to me? Her laughter had a bit of a haunting truth to it. I dropped the subject.

Once in the kitchen, I kicked into an unthinking, programmed, late-night mode. Zombiesk, I went to the refrigerator and opened the door; not really hungry, not really even knowing what I was looking for…if anything. Of course, had I actually been a zombie, the choice would have been obvious, brains.

I sensed her before I even knew I was being watched. Just one of those feelings, like something in the room has changed. I slowly turned from the door and glanced under my armpit. About five paces from my feet, eerily illuminated by the faint glow of the low-watt bulb, *sat* an ordinary brown mouse.

Though peculiar, I feel I have accurately described the rodent's posture by stating she was *seated*. She was leaned against the cupboard with her bottom to the floor and her two tiny feet stretched out in front. In her hands she was holding what looked like part of a potato…and she was staring right at me. She looked as if she had been there for hours; waiting…for me? I held the eye-contact for just a brief moment before turning, closing the fridge and stepping to the light switch on the far wall. The act took no more than three seconds, but when I looked back, she was gone.

I knew she was female after an encounter with a rogue male last summer while cleaning out a shed near the woods. It is not an overstatement to suggest I was ambushed. I cracked open the door to sweep the floor when from a shelf he leapt at my neck; not unlike the fanged rabbit from Monty Python's Holy Grail. He looked to tear out my jugular. I was able to get a hold of him as he death-gripped the collar of my shirt, steadying himself for the fatal blow. I squeezed him tight and flung him as hard as I could against a window on the adjacent side. The window cracked from the force and he slid to the floor...and died. I was breathing heavy from the battle and as I walked over to observe my worthy opponent I saw, fittingly, his testicles were far too large for his body. If I were equally endowed I would have two bowling balls nestled between my thighs. Needless to say I felt as if my victory had merit.

She, of the kitchen, was lacking said equipment. Plus, on the sparsely-haired belly I thought I made out a bunch of nipples, lined single-file as if waiting at customs.

I moved to the cupboard and discovered the small, raw potato lying on the floor where she had just been. I bent over and picked it up; it was a cube from this morning when I had made fresh hash browns. My next move was one I will never be able to explain to any one rational; I plopped it in my mouth and began to chew. I did it without a second thought as to Hana virus or rat-scratch fever...or rabies...or whatever. I swallowed, turned the light off, and went back to bed. I was relaxed and happy and instantly fell asleep; not waking until morning.

Debate, Puppies, Trouble and Tit Shots

Sleeplessness has become a way of life. Once awake it is as if an automatic coffeemaker has been turned on, filling my brain in a steady stream of "things to be done." It has always been this way for me. I tell my students this and they seem to like the idea that I am up and *on duty* for them. I coach high school debate and forensics, which has nothing to do with dead bodies, but rather is competitive acting and speech. Some of my best ideas flood my mind at 2:00am. Properly motivated, I could link the purchase of a piece of Laffy-Taffy to economic collapse and the eventual extinction of the planet via nuke war…of course this is only the second worst scenario; just behind the final horseman of the apocalypse, *dehumanization*; though I only suppose a debater would find humor in that.

The general program I run is: Lie in bed for about half an hour trying to convince myself, I can *will* myself back to sleep. I focus on a small black box and nothing else…that nothingness actually sometimes works, but rarely. I start thinking about *thinking about nothing* and that damn black box. After I have done due diligence to return to slumber, I get out of bed and move to the living room. Sometimes my wife wakes and asks what's wrong and sometimes she does not and sometimes I just know she is fake-sleeping, but neither she nor I really care. I usually wake Zeke as I pass by and he follows me out to the couch, my destination. I might make a stop by the toilet as I am beginning to suspect my prostate has grown. I am awakened more and more by the sensation of a full bladder. I put off having it checked as my doctor has thick fingers. I noticed this as we shook hands one Sunday at Wal-Mart. Thick fingers and big hands; the exam could wait.

In the living room, I often sit in the dark. I do a lot of reminiscing with myself there. On one such night, while sitting in the dark on the couch, lost in deep thought, I was reminded of a Christmas morning when I was just about seven years old. This Christmas had several *keeper,* mental, Polaroid moments I would tuck away. As it happens with me way too often, on this particular Christmas, I had a mental break with reality.

I woke early that Christmas morning and snuck my way to the living room, alone. We were by no means a wealthy family. At this time in my life, we lived in a 10X55 foot trailer. But, as with any family with great parents, the issue of money was never an issue. We simply were loved and taught to be proud of who we were, so… we were.

I remember my trailer park years fondly for the most part. I did have what I called, *the Miss Woodle incident* that traumatized me for years though. I had contracted measles and was unable to go to school for a few days and then *refused* to go to school for days after on account of my appearance. I must have been vain for a child or maybe it is normal to not want to be seen by your friends covered in hundreds of small red dots. Even at an early age, kids can be quite creative with their ridicule. I wasn't sure exactly what would be said, but even at seven I could come up with several words that rhymed with *scab*. I was miserable.

I remember lying in bed naked, covered head to toe with Calamine lotion. My memory is fuzzy on the details, but the gist of the *incident* was, after a few days my teacher, Miss Woodle, came to visit me to see how I was doing. I don't really remember Miss Woodle in the classroom, and if not for this *incident*, she might have been gone from my memory forever. I can assume she was a caring teacher though, as not many would come to a student's home to check on them.

This is how my mind plays it back to me. My mom calls to me from the living room that my teacher has come to visit me. I refuse to come out due to embarrassment. My mother works her guilt, magic magnet, and like a piece of steel, I am pulled from my bed to the next room. Standing before my teacher, I say, "Hi Miss Woodle." I remember her looking at me strange…my mom looking at me strange…a long pause…too long. The silence is broken by my dear mother shouting, "BRIAN!" It took me a moment…but the shock of her voice heightened my conscientiousness and made me realize something that had slipped my mind. I was standing before my teacher, Miss Woodle, completely naked. The memory ends there.

On Christmas Eve, my two brothers and I slept in the same room. Brad was eight and Johnny was three. We would normally stay up as late as we could on that night. From the open bedroom door we could see the random flashes of illumination dancing shadows in hallway; lights that were strung on a too-large-for-the-trailer, cedar tree. Always a free, misshaped, cedar tree cut from the timber of some unsuspecting land owner. The overpowering scent would fill the house and although very reminiscent of cat piss…it eventually became the odor I most associated with the holiday.

Though we all had our own beds, we would all crawl into just one and whisper about Santa and giggle. Then we would play puppies. It is almost embarrassing to describe the activity to others as it will just appear queer; and you can take that however you wish. We would get under the covers and crawl around making…well, puppy sounds. We would mimic puppy actions too: rolling across each other, snuggling and sniffing butts. I am being honest when I tell you it truly was a grand memory and maybe, just maybe, the world has become so tainted with cruel words and fear of what other might think that playing puppies just seems stupid now.

But, on this particular night, post-puppy play, while my brothers slumbered, I ventured to the couch and sat alone just opposite the tree. There is nothing more magical than sitting in complete silence, staring at the beautiful blinking lights from a Christmas tree playing umbrella to a shag carpet full of presents. At that point in my life, I was an all-out believer in Santa. So, I reasoned I had just missed him; a definite magic multiplier. I could still smell his aftershave, *Brute*, just like my dad's. Here is where my mental break occurred.

Every child knows the unwritten law of present opening. You wait as long as possible, then at the first sign of light you wake your parents, and together you all gather around the tree and disperse the presents in some manner; but not this Christmas. I sat there alone with a smile on my face. There was a slight chill as a winter draft wandered about the trailer, but snug in my Hong Kong Phooey pajamas, I was protected enough as to not be distracted.

I looked about the tree spotting many of the contributions I had made hanging from glue-glopped yarn on various branches. Our tree was unique in the fact that all the decorations were man-made, well, *boy*-made. Intermittently speckled between the popcorn garland, which was strung just nights before while watching Hee Haw and sipping hot cocoa, hung cotton-faced Santas and pipe-cleaner reindeer.

Each year my mother, who was in no way artistic or crafty, would construct a make-shift, ornament assembly line on the kitchen table. I am not sure where she came up with the ideas; she sure wasn't Googling them in 1974. We would look across the table filled with cotton balls, construction paper, glue, glitter, crayons, tooth picks, buttons, hole-punchers, and popcorn…just an endless list of diverse items to be used in the construction. It was at this table, year after year, we would generate the objects that would later adorn the tree, and make it truly one of a kind; the Weilert family Christmas tree.

To this day, I still have a green, corduroy wreath with red, hole-punched berries and the name BRIAN poorly scrawled across the back hanging from our artificial tree; the wreath, an archaic stranger amongst the shiny, new, store-bought balls. To my shame, I wasn't able to generate neither the motivation nor the energy to recreate this seemingly simple time my mother so effortlessly set aside to create special Christmas memories with my own kids.

Without really thinking, a habit I struggle with, I rose from the couch and went to the gifts. I moved them about quietly as to not wake anyone. I finally came to a present with my name. I began feeling about the paper trying to discern its content. There had been little effort to hide its shape and I could tell there was a hard oval on the top center. As I pushed on it, a loud 'POP' noise was made. It scared me at first and I dropped it. After a brief recovery time, I picked it back up and did it again. I had to know what the heck it was…again I wasn't thinking, so I opened it up. It was the game of *Trouble*. You push a clear plastic half dome with dice in the center, and it recoils back up, thus rolling the dice…of course with that satisfying 'POP'. Within a few minutes, I had managed my way through the instructions and for the most part had figured out how to play. I set it up for two players and began to 'POP' and move my cone-shaped pieces around the board. Lost to me was the clear violation of Christmas rules and the sound I was generating with each turn. Heck, I don't know, I might have even been talking to myself in two voices as I played the role of a competitor. I was completely lost in my enjoyment; lost, until my mom's voice, "Brian! What do you think you are doing?!" Much like *the Woodle incident*, I had a sudden realization of just exactly what I *was* doing. I had no explanation.

Here is where reality and memory differ. Years later, when my mother told the story, she claimed it was not Christmas Eve, but rather a week before Christmas and the gift was from my Grandma...not Santa. To this day I dispute this as there is no way I would do something like that...even at seven. However, I can leave a small bit of room she might be correct.

I have learned many memories from childhood can blend and blur into an inconceivable, fuzzy timeline. For example, as a child I had an *issue*. I can't blame it on a faulty prostate as I would now, as I was maybe three or four at the time. But, I never seemed to be able to get all the dribbles out before tucking my peter away and as a result, the fronts of my pants were always a bit damp. I also had a habit of touching my privates...maybe due to the discomfort of the wetness. Nonetheless, by the end of a day of playing outside, whatever I happened to be wearing below the waist, was coated with pee-mud. It was a constant embarrassment for Mom. I know she thought the neighbors would think she was a bad mother for letting her child run around the neighborhood looking like that. On more than one occasion, I remember being scolded for playing with myself and for being seen out and about looking the way I did. The thing is, I don't ever remember it ever really bothering me.

The whole reason I bring this up is that to me, this memory also takes place in the trailer park. But, at three, we didn't live in a trailer park....So, either I was seven when this occurred, something I can't fathom, or my mom just might be right about *Trouble.*

One Christmas memory I am clear on, and could years later verify via 8mm film, was the tit-shot. I am not sure when we acquired the camera, but once in my parent's possession most events of importance, and many which were not, from then forward were caught on film. I remember watching film of the time when I was put into judo. I don't ever really remember asking to be in judo. It must have just seemed natural...living a trailer park...it made one think of the beautiful Orient and of course, martial arts. Besides being able to watch myself compete via film, my only real memory of this activity was my first encounter with breast feeding. Now, before going further, I need to point out this is not the afore mentioned tit-shot referenced...but I will get around to that.

The feeding incident involved a teammate named Jose. Now this is a memory I feel confident about until I bring to light he was black. Not that a black child from the south cannot have Hispanic heritage...but Jose didn't. Jose was around my age; which of course is a topic of some dispute during my time in the trailer. But, no matter my age, it doesn't change the discomfort I felt when I watched Jose walk from the mat after a match, directly to his mother; a very large woman with each boob the size of a laundry bag a college kid might drag home on the weekend.

Upon seeing her son approach and apparently sensing his parchment from his bout, she unleashed one of the monstrosities from beneath her blouse and allowed him to quench his thirst. I don't have to go into much detail as I feel the image has been painted...I could see Bob Ross on PBS bringing the image to life with a, "And over here we will put a happy little breast." Except it wasn't little, Bob! It was massive; an abstract work of art permanently hanging askew in the gallery of my brain. Watching a bipedal mammal moving under its own power to suckle from a teat is just haunting.

My mom tried to explain to me how natural the whole ordeal was, but her twisted face gave away the lie and we let it pass with a hidden understanding that this is something I should never, ever attempt...even if I were dying of thirst.

Other memories were also captured on the grainy, hiccupped film produced from the state-of-the-art camera: baseball games, pushing toy cars off the roof to watch them explode onto the hard ground, mud fights...and of course the tit-shot. I am not sure any child should see his mother's breast after a certain age, unless, of course, you are Jose. It seems as if it could be damaging in some way, scarring one for life.

But, on this Christmas, this Christmas of *Trouble*, I would not be spared. My father was the cinematographer, moving about as we opened presents. We all were busy, lost in the art of separating paper from product...we were playing our substantial roles in this holiday docudrama. My mother sat with nothing to do but watch...so, when my father whipped the camera in her direction, void of any script, she improvised. It happened without thought, perhaps revealing the origins of my own shortcomings. It began with a crooked little grin that was a trademark of Mom right before being ornery. Then, with a flash, she pulled her boob from her nightgown and just as quickly tucked it away. I could tell she was immediately embarrassed, but it was too late. My father, who thought the whole episode was a delight, ran from her as she tried to erase the bizarre moment from the camera. To this day, I know I have the film hiding away in a box.

But, I was wrong; it didn't emotionally scar me in any way. It is a reminder of the playfulness my parents shared. A reminder of just how much they loved each other. A love we children didn't really understand, but its runoff poured onto us and made our lives happy. On more than one occasion, my father made it clear where he stood. He would proclaim to never make him choose between Mom or us. He would remind us, he *chose* her, and if we were to disappear…well, he could always make more children.

The Second Encounter

We are taught at an early age that mice are dirty and a sure sign someone isn't keeping up on housework. To that I would have two comments: One, is the mouse I witnessed for the second time, seemed as if she were fresh from the shower. And two, my wife is responsible for cleaning the house.

It had been about a week since my last encounter. In fact, I had been in such a dazed stupor the time before I wasn't really sure it all wasn't some crazy dream. Unless watching a Saturday morning cartoon, where else can you catch a glimpse of a rodent so properly seated? My basic routine differed on this evening. Instead of going to the refrigerator for food or the couch for TV or pondering, I wandered off to the bathroom medicine cabinet.

Many years ago I had been diagnosed with gout. Now, for those not familiar with this affliction, I will try to put it in laymen's terms. However, before going into detail, I feel it is best to start with the most obvious for those who share in this exclusive society; it hurts like hell! The best I can describe it is…it feels like someone has shoved a small shard of glass into the joints of my big toes, or feet, or ankles, or knees…and just recently my elbows. Gout is like a booty-call from a porcupine…it shows up in the middle of the night and of course, besides the shock value of, "What the hell is a porcupine doing in the suburbs?", it's painful. Unless, of course you're into that sort of thing and then the whole metaphor just falls apart.

Quick medical lesson for anyone out there in denial…you know who you are…you, who wakes up in the middle of the night and says, "Hmmmm, I don't remember breaking my foot." You have gout! Your body produces a high amount of uric acid and cannot process it…so, it forms into hard crystals that apparently love to nestle into places where they would cause the most pain. It is called the rich man's disease as the foods and drink kings consumed were high in uric acid and many a royalty suffered from this affliction. But, don't worry, you are in good company. Benjamin Franklin not only suffered from it, but also wrote an essay to his gout. I, unfortunately, am one of a small group of *goutist*, a word I just might trademark, who come by their uric acid the old fashioned way; genetics.

There are a million home remedies out there…so read up; eat cherries and celery seed by the handfuls…maybe it will help. I haven't had great luck. I do know, every time I have a flare up, my joints never fully recover and this chronic burden is crippling me...slowly...so, slowly I can still lie to myself that it isn't happening.

At the medicine cabinet, I find some anti-inflammatory pill; usually a knock-off brand that pretends to be *Aleve* or *Tylenol*. When you come from a family like mine, you grow up frugal...or as my wife and kids prefer, *cheap*. As I moved to the sink to get a glass of water, I didn't notice her at first...or maybe she moved into position after I had already visually scanned the soap dish. Nonetheless, as I turned on the water, she was less than two inches from my hand.

I am not sure why we even had a soap dish. The sink has two concave sea-shells on either side of the faucet where the soap was supposed to be placed...it just seemed redundant. I reacted like a school girl who just realized the creepy kid in science class had put a tarantula on her shoulder...yes, I screamed...or squealed; some feminine sound I hadn't heard escape my mouth before.

The mouse didn't move; didn't flinch. And this is where this whole thing starts to read like a fable...I swear on my mother's grave, the damn thing was smiling. I thought to swat at her, but that smile took me off guard and set me in a direction that flirted with insanity. I smiled back. But, as soon as I did, I realized the mouse wasn't smiling...maybe never was...and I felt a fool. So, there we were, the mouse and I, her *maybe* having reached out to communicate with some sort of human gesture, and I with my foot pounding in pain truly at a loss as to how to proceed. Some time passed. I'm not sure how long, as in situations such as these, it is hard to tell...though to be honest I have never been in a Mexican standoff with a rodent before as to gage how time might be disrupted…However, I do wonder if using terms like *Mexican standoff* is racist. I hope not. Maybe if the mouse had been Speedy Gonzales it wouldn't be...or else it would exacerbate the issue.

I remember when I first used that word, *exacerbate*, in my debate class. It is a term that appears in a lot of evidence to show how problems can be linked to create bigger problems or impacts. But, to a teen's mind unfamiliar with the word, it just sounds a lot like *masturbate*. So, every time it is first introduced, it is followed by uncontrolled giggles. It is nice to hear cynical, high school students can still giggle. I usually let it pass without comment and then continue; partially because it does sound a little dirty every time I say it. Scatological references are also still funny to them. Anything that might tie to a bodily function is cause for the same giggles...though the words *poop* or *pee* rarely appear in serious research.

So, after an undetermined period of time, I felt some action was needed. It had become both too awkward and just plain weird. I spoke to her.

"What's up little lady?"

I sounded calm and friendly. I had owned two rodents in my life. Well, I owned one and my oldest son had one for a time. Mine was a gerbil I had acquired after playing the role of Jonathon Harker in the play *Dracula*. It was supposed to be a mouse playing the role of Cuthbert, but someone owned the gerbil and was looking to get rid of him. Cuthbert was apparently a bit of an escape artist and they had grown weary of his unique talent. After the play concluded, I took him home as a pet. I had control of him for about a week before he disappeared. I went to his cage one morning and he was gone. I caught a glimpse of him about a month later sprinting down the hallway late in the evening. I didn't give chase. I figured he was enjoying what was left of his short existence as a free man.

My son's mouse was all white and named *Ghost*. I don't remember why we acquired him, but can guess he just wanted one and since they were sold as food for snakes, *Ghost* was cheap. Plus, I still had the cage left over from Cuthbert. The white mouse did not last long as a Weilert family pet. One evening my son sat him on the ground and he tried to scamper off. I instinctively stomped my foot. He rolled over and died. My son, who is now in his mid-twenties, to this day believes I missed the mouse and *Ghost* just died of a heart attack. Maybe he believes this because he could not face the fact his father would stomp on his pet. Maybe he believes it because I said, I missed him and he died of a heart attack.

"What's up little lady?" seemed to do the trick as she moved in my direction a full two steps, or about one inch. I slowly lowered my hand. I wasn't sure what I expected... yes I did…I was expecting some Dr. Doolittle moment where she would crawl onto my palm and we would be lifelong friends. What happened was she bolted; leaping from the sink and shooting between my legs to disappear into the living room. My first thought was, how can animals jump from such great distances without being hurt? I mean, with some rough calculations, I would guess the height would be equivalent to me plummeting from a twenty story building. If I were to do that, I would splatter like a large lawn-and-leaf bag filled with vegetable beef stew. I most definitely wouldn't land lightly on my feet and have the ability to sprint. Nimble bitch...I grabbed an icepack from the freezer for my foot, and wandered back to bed.

I Won't Say Goodbye

My mother always beamed with pride when she told others that not one, but all three of her boys grew up to be teachers. She worked as a secretary in a middle school and knew how important positive role models were for those who had none. She would often tell me of times she would pull troubled kids close and give them the "tough love" she dealt all those years to her own children. She would often joke they would probably fire her because it wasn't her job. But, they didn't fire her and years rolled by with her helping child after child that came through her office angry, confused and in need of something she innately possessed. Besides extremely short legs, this ability was the most prominent thing she passed on to her children.

I left the classroom in her final year alive. I had earned my masters and felt I owed it to myself to use the degree…so I became a principal. It was toward the end of the school year when she passed. It would be an understatement to say I felt as if my life had no purpose. I have since left that position and went back to the classroom. I needed that connection with kids again. If just for a while, I needed to do the thing again my mother said all her kids were born to do, teach.

The pain from my mother's death is still hard to bear. I have always been very closed with my feelings. My mother shared this trait. Situations where others would cry, Mom and I would talk about why we didn't feel the need. It wasn't as if we didn't hurt, we did, but it just manifested itself differently. Some people would call us cold hearted, but they would be very wrong. I can't tell you how often I wanted to cry since her passing, but I just don't. She would not begrudge me this.

My mother had a condition that caused her heart to enlarge, in turn causing her valves to leak. She was on medication to shrink the heart in hopes the leaking would stop. It slowed, but did not stop. She would walk miles every night and pray very hard to be healed, but it just wasn't getting the job done. A decision had to be made. She always panicked at the thought of not being able to do all the things she could before. She was an active, vibrant soul and to her, the thought of being less was unbearable. If she did not have an operation she would live, many years perhaps, but the condition would at some point worsen and finally she would be incapacitated and die. Or she could have open-heart surgery to fix the problem. She prayed some more and her and my father decided to go ahead with the surgery.

My father hated hospitals. Years earlier he had watched as his own father faded while confined in the glorified hollows of a hospital; watched as his father was misdiagnosed and died.

Mom told him it was all in God's hands and who could argue with that? Mom and I joked before the operation, if she died, it would make a great story for me. We laughed, but it wasn't genuine. She was very afraid.

As my two brothers, sister, and father joined at the hospital on the day of the surgery everything seemed to be going just fine. I never even entertained the thought of a mishap. Mom would be fine and home in a few days and we would all celebrate for the next twenty to thirty years…Hell, she might outlive us all. Hours into the surgery, when she was supposed to be out, the nurse called down to the waiting room and told us it would be longer, but everything was going fine. I watched Dad's face as he got off the phone. He was shaken. This is a man who had been through so much in his life, and had never shown distress. I began to worry. I could spend hours telling of the loving relationship between my parents, high school sweethearts, who were bonded in a way I have seen no other couple. But, you will just have to take my word on it.

Mom did come out of surgery, an hour or so later than expected. When she was finally moved to her room, we all breathed a sigh of relief. Over the next few hours she was talking and seemed to be doing great. We all spoke with her, but nothing meaningful as we would all be back in the morning and she would be doing even better by then. So, at around 9:00 pm, all of us children went home to sleep at

Mom and Dad's house an hour away. My dad stayed. I told myself, "See, there was nothing to worry about."

We had just gotten into bed when we got the call. She had thrown a blood clot and we needed to come. We all raced back to the hospital where we found our dad down where they performed CAT scans. He was lost. What would he do without her? The clot had caused some bleeding in the brain, a stroke. They moved her back to ICU. From this point on I am haunted by memories of the remaining time I had to spend with the woman who made me who I am. My older brother, Brad, was alone in the ICU room with her, keeping the family vigil. Hours passed and he came to get me. He was crying, "I can't do it anymore." By the look of his face, this wasn't just a feeling, but a fact. He was emotionally and physically drained. It was my turn. Alone with Mom, I sat by her side. It was quiet. The only sounds were the artificial interrupted beeps from the machine that spat out vitals: blood pressure, heart rate, and respiration. Mom would go periods of several seconds where she wouldn't breathe. I would panic and shake her shoulders, "Breathe Mom, breathe," and she would again.

When she woke, she wanted out of bed and kept trying to sit up. "I just want to get up. Why can't I just get up?" As she moved, the left side of her body was immobile. Her words were slurred as one side of her face was drooped, paralyzed. I still thought she was going to live and the thoughts of her telling me she would never want to be like this broke me. I cried as I held her down on the bed. "Mom, you've had a stroke, you can't get up."

"I can too! You just need to help me. Why won't you help me? Brad would help me if he was here."

"No Mom you can't!" I raised my voice trying to sound stern. I wanted so badly to let her up, but I knew her struggle to stand could make things worse.

I'm not sure how long this went on, but too long. The timeline here gets blurred as if I were in an alternate universe. I know my dad came in and I left. Sometime later he came out, frantic. "She threw another clot!" We all raced down to the CAT scan once again. It was then everything in our world fell apart. They informed us she had massive bleeding in the brain and was in a coma.

Our extended family had come to the hospital some time earlier and were all gathered in the waiting room. My father pulled all of his children together and searched our eyes for an *okay* to the decision he and Mom had worked out long before this moment. We all prayed together, hands interlocked....and agreed.

They took her off the respirator. *Fixed*, her heart was strong now. So, Mom's heart kept beating, but the woman we all knew and loved was gone. Everyone took turns, one at a time, to say goodbyes, all but me. No one noticed, so caught up in the torment of their own pain. I just couldn't. If I said goodbye, this horrible nightmare was true, it was all over and...I just couldn't. Dad, in the wake of the most tragic event of his life, still worried about us kids as he specifically asked me if I had had the chance to tell Mom goodbye. He said it was important. I lied. We were all together, Mom's whole family, her whole life, when she took her last breath.

How do you say goodbye forever to your mother? How? I couldn't…wouldn't.

6

The Third Encounter

The mouse and I were sitting on the back porch,
overlooking the water, and we were smoking pipes. The
conversation was sparse as we sat mostly in silence
enjoying the view. When the mouse spoke it was to inquire
about my wife and children. She seemed very interested in
them. I don't remember the words, just the feeling of
genuine concern and love. I responded with deep thoughts
about my failings as a father and husband, words I had
never spoken while awake. She assured me I had done a
fine job and then blew a smoke ring that grew and
expanded to surround the entire lake. We laughed some,
though I cannot recall specifics as to why; I just know it
had been some time since I was this happy. As I watched

the smoke circle grow, I had a sense of peace. Zeke farted and I awoke…it was 3:00 am.

Hidden Skidmarks

When I finished five years in the Coast Guard, I decided to
return back to Kansas to go to college. When I had left, I
was wild, single, lost as to what my life would hold, and
was sure as hell never coming back to Kansas to live.
When I returned, I was a stable father and husband who
knew he wanted to be a teacher…in Kansas. The year I
returned my two brothers and my father decided they
wanted to do a *father son turkey hunt*. It sounded like a
great bonding adventure…except, I didn't hunt. My
suggestion of going someplace warm to golf was rejected.
They knew of the time I spent with Mom in the kitchen and
of my cooking prowess and stroked my ego by saying,
"You don't have to hunt, you can be the camp bitch and
just cook for us." Ah, how could I refuse such flattery?

So, we went.

Each great journey begins with a single step and this step
led to a string of twenty-three consecutive turkey
adventures…and still counting; each loaded with memories
to fill volumes. After my first year as the gender
derogatory *bitch*, I learned to hunt. We had years where
the trip was in jeopardy. The year my mother passed was
just such a year. None of us felt as if we could muster the
energy to attend. But, my mother, who had sacrificed her
anniversary with my father each year so we could go
because she knew the importance of us staying connected,
would have been disappointed in us. So, we went.
Illnesses, injury, family and work troubles were never
allowed to derail this sacred weekend. If we could go the
year of my mother's death, we would never miss it again.

These past few years we were hunting up north. My
younger brother Johnny and I lived in southeast Kansas and
had taken up the habit of driving up together. We would
get out of school on Thursday and drive up for a Friday,
Saturday, Sunday hunt. The year of writing this book, my
brother decided he would not leave until Friday morning. I
am a creature of habit, and this curveball was something at
which I didn't want to swing. I decided to apply some of
my well-practice guilt I had learned from Mom. I even
used her death as a device to drive shame into him for
depriving us of the travel time together to catch up on our
lives. I said something like *Mom would have been
disappointed in his decision.* Mom would have approved
of this tactic. However, when this maneuver failed, I was
forced to go to code red, and just outright highjack his
humility. That blackmail is what gave birth to this chapter.

Sometimes you just have to shoot a hostage to show you mean business.

On the Wednesday before we were to leave, I emailed Johnny the remaining words of this chapter with the threat of, "This will be chapter seven if we don't leave on Thursday." I took a few liberties with the truth to ramp up his discomfort of not departing on the day I desired. He read it and replied with a threat of his own of writing a book too. He attached the first chapter which simply read: *My brother is an S.O.B.* He claimed chapter two was well on its way. In the end he chose to not acquiesce to my demand…and so, I present to you, Chapter seven:

My father worked as a boilermaker, which is to say he traveled around the country welding. We moved often. Before I was ten, I had lived in ten states. On these moves the living arrangements varied from house to house. Due to our travels, there were occasions I would room with my older brother…sometimes with my younger…sometimes I had my own room and there were times all three of us shared a room.

During one particular summer, we moved to a country home in Illinois. At this old farm house, I was selected to room with my younger brother John Weilert, who we all call Johnny. Johnny was four years my junior. He was a quiet kid who seldom played with the guys. While my older brother, Brad, and I would ride our little 50cc Indian motorcycle for hours upon hours, only breaking during the time *Speed Racer* would air, Johnny would remain inside. Johnny had a peculiar attraction to dolls and would dress them up and move them about our room playing out some creepy, adolescent soap opera. Many times I would come back to the room to find my poor GI Joe humiliated, stripped of his weapons and wearing a dress. But, since Mom had always wanted a girl, he was allowed to do so. My father spoke little, but his furrowed brow and the shake of his head spoke volumes.

About mid-summer, in the heat of July, I began to notice a strong odor in the room. My family was always very frugal and so air-conditioning was not an option. I complained to the management, but both Mom and Dad said it was probably just a dead mouse in the walls and it would go away in a week or so...it didn't. As we approached August, the smell had become unbearable. My second complaint was lodged; this time my mother took notice. Her change of heart had less to do with my persuasive presentation and more to do with an odd occurrence, Johnny was out of underwear.

CSI was not needed as Mom took care of the investigation. She soon discovered the cause of odiferous emanation...Johnny had been having a problems with getting a clean wipe and had been leaving skidmarks in his *tighty-whities*. Embarrassed a six year old would lack the control; he decided hiding them was a viable option to putting them in the laundry and facing the ridicule. He was truly impressive. His cover-up knew no bounds.
Mom allowed me to play her consigliore and we slowly found the discarded undergarments one by one. It must have been the same feeling the police had when uncovering bodies in a serial killers crawlspace. He had stuffed them under the mattress, beneath the toy box, behind the curtains, shoved them in the toes of seldom used boots...time has erased many of the locations from my

memory, but I to this day remain in awe. All told, some fifteen pairs of underwear, all distinctly marked with the same *M.O.,* were unearthed.

As I informed Johnny his story would appear in the book, he asked me to at least counterbalance it with the fact he has a huge schlong. I told him I would indeed lie for him and include that fact.

Johnny has a huge schlong.

8

The Fourth Encounter

Along with debate, I coached wrestling for a number of years. My wife's mom hated the fact I would leave her daughter alone on weekends to go to tournaments. Her husband was a man who worked at a wastewater treatment plant across the street. He was punctual. A man with few friends or hobbies, he was home at the same time every night. I think she expected the same for her daughter.

So, it was fitting she passed away on the night before I was to leave for the regional tournament. I don't mean to sound crass, but she had a great sense of humor and would not begrudge me that comment.

I took the phone call about Anna's death from my wife's brother in our basement apartment. The same apartment where just a year ago she had sat late one night laughing as she made fun of her husband who was screaming from the guest room to turn the TV volume down to an oddly specific twenty-two. Dick, my father-in-law is a very particular man. Whereas my dad operated under the belief, "By gosh if duct tape works on a repair…well it works," Dick was more along the line of calling in engineers to create a design to later be drawn up by architects and implemented by a group of experts. And that was to just change a light bulb.

Anna was an obedient, caring wife so, to hear her let loose about his antics on this particular night was out of the norm which heightened the humor for us all. She loved to make people happy. My wife and I have a picture of her dressed as a clown. It was something she did every year to entertain the students at the school where she worked. Anna took the remote and pointed it at the television repeating, through now nearly uncontrolled laughter, "Two, Two." Now, my wife seated on the very couch, would have to burden the worst news she had ever heard…and I drew the short straw.

I managed to stay stoic as I told her. I knew I had to be strong. My mom was a veteran at keeping it together and I inherited the trait. My wife called me a liar; screamed it repeatedly, "LIAR, LIAR!" My heart broke for her as she eventually collapsed into me, crippled with grief.
We headed to New York for the funeral and went through all the horrible things associated with such an event. Dick was lost, so my wife had to handle everything. I was by her side as she listened to the used-car-salesman funeral

home director tell her about the various coffin accessories as if he were peddling a used Buick. He was a kind man; the kind I wanted to beat to death. At one point he actually told my wife she could go with the less expensive vault, but in a few years it would fail and worms would get to her mother's body.

When we returned to her childhood home an eerie occurrence happened. All of the flowers and plants from the funeral had been brought into the living room. Attached to one of the plants was a Mylar, helium-filled balloon. Somehow, the balloon had broken loose from its bondage and was floating free. It didn't fly to the ceiling pushing like a sparrow trying to escape through a skylight, but rather hovered midway in space about head-high. That in itself was bizarre. Why would a new balloon behave in such a manner? But, what followed, was even *more* bizarre.

As my wife walked around the house, the balloon seemed to follow her. One could argue the breeze created by her movement caused a draft…in which the balloon only behaved as a balloon. But, as it followed her down the hallway when she headed off to bed, I was convinced it was her mother. I told her of my suspicions, but she showed no desire to get sucked into the insanity of my thinking…and went to sleep. I was left alone in the living room with that damn balloon that had somehow made its way back to me.

So, when I saw the mouse for the third time, my mind wandered back to the time with the balloon… could my mom be reaching out to me? Could this damn mouse be her? I didn't mentally or emotionally make the connection as a concrete belief, but I would be lying if I didn't admit it was like a first grader hiding under the bed with his legs sticking out. It was there, hidden…and I knew it.

I was once again in the kitchen, and I as I switched on the lights, I saw her over by the garbage. It was Wednesday and tomorrow was trash day so, I appreciated the reminder. I had a habit of forgetting and then had to deal with an abundance of waste. It is unbelievable the amount of refuse two people can create in just six days. If I wasn't up nearly every evening, I would swear my wife was sneaking out and filling up the cans with papers she collected from our neighbors.

The mouse, as always, must have anticipated my arrival. She was up on her hind feet stretching toward me. Again, I know I sound crazy, and maybe I am, but she was moving her hands in what could be interpreted as a wave. From here on, the mouse encounters will just flat out read as silly fiction, but I can only put to paper what happened to the best of my memory.

The mouse dropped to all fours and moved toward me. I do want to point out it was very late or very early and my mind was cloudy. Or maybe, I just want to believe it, so I seemed less…I don't know…nuts? I chose to ignore her at first. At that point, I didn't want to acknowledge the metaphorical legs protruding from the bed, so I broke eye contact and headed for the comfort zone of the refrigerator. I focused hard on the lunchmeat selection trying to disregard the fact an over-friendly mouse might be at this very moment perched atop one of my Hobbit feet. I was actually panicked. Even if I were to let my mind entertain

the fact it might in some way be my mother, how freaky
was that? I was afraid if I looked down she just might say,
"Brian, do you really need to be eating this late?"

The year before her death, I had, to borrow a word from a
previous chapter, ballooned to nearly 260 pounds. At that
point she was walking ten miles a day to strengthen her
heart. She was still stocky but firm. I too had been larger
than most. The first pair of jeans I remember her buying
for me were JC Penny Plain Pockets with the reinforced
knees. The size? Husky. My older brother, who could pass
for an emaciated Chihuahua, relished in the fact my
clothing actually had the word *husky* on the label. I
suppose the world had yet to discover political correctness
in the textile industry.

When Mom would see me at the many family gatherings, a
thing that dwindled with her death, she would remark how
she was concerned I might just drop from a heart attack.
She was brutally honest with me, but it was always coated
with a thick layer of love to cushion the blow. I told her
the same words I told my dad as he awkwardly tried to
deliver the *birds and the bees* talk… "I know! I know!"
Side note: At ten you do not want to hear your father say
words such as: *pussy, cock*…and I kid you not, though I
tried to forget, *blowing your load.* Apparently, he failed to
read any Dr. Spock before the endeavor; a blue collar talk
from a blue collar man.

Back in the fridge, I looked over the selection of cold cuts.
There was sun-dried tomato, infused turkey that was
delicious, but it was smashed against the back wall by the

milk container and I couldn't remember when I had bought it...so a risk was involved.

As I pondered the decision, I gathered my courage and turned my head to locate the mouse. I thought she had gone and I was a bit relieved, but a motion drew my attention closer and I realized she within inches of my slippers...standing. I froze. What the hell? Right? She wasn't making any aggressive maneuvers, so my heart beat slowed...a bit.

We stood there looking at each other for too long to be considered polite. I slowly reached deep into fridge blindly trying to retrieve the turkey. I didn't take my eyes off of her and she returned the favor. Once in hand, I took off the wrapper and pulled a small piece from a corner and threw it to the floor. It landed amongst the toe-hair atop my footwear. She slowly moved toward me and blindly reached for the turkey...she didn't take her eyes off of me and I returned the favor. Once in hand, she took her small piece from the corner and dropped to the *normal* mouse stance, looked away, and walked back to the garbage. She paused for just a second as if she wanted to say something, but didn't look back...then disappeared behind trash can. I took this as a clear sign from God...the turkey was okay to eat. So, I made a sandwich.

Orange Cattle-Beast and Porcupine Meatballs

I am having a hard time adjusting to cooking for just Stacia and myself. First, I learned how to cook from Mom and she always overcooked for the sake of having leftovers the next day so she wouldn't have to cook lunch…a two for one deal. So, I struggle to not cook as if we are having a rugby team for supper every night. In case you are interested, that is fifteen people. Second, without kids we don't eat on the same schedule. We eat when we are hungry now, and my wife is a notorious *snacker*, as a result, she never really is. I will cook a wonderful dinner only to hear her say; she wished I would have waited…as she's not hungry. Well, stop eating the damn pretzels and onion dip and you would be! I shouldn't complain as I should be used to this type of schedule.

Growing up it was really difficult to put our family eating habits into a norm. When my father was home we would always have hand-prepared, sit-down meals at the dining table. When he traveled, it seemed as if all of my mother's energy was spent dealing with her children; more specifically, me. As a result, when it came to meals she seldom cooked. I remember bologna... cheap fish sticks, which always had *that one* with the dark brown strip that tasted super-fishy; waiting to ambush your unsuspecting taste buds like a culinary game of Russian roulette...or hotdogs which were ironically eaten as cold, uncooked afternoon snacks, and hot...as , appropriately named hot-dog suppers...boxed Mac-n-cheese that would span from a too-runny, yellow-orange milk to a sticky paste that fused to make one globule on the plate...an endless revolution of TV dinners that assured us of a well-balanced meal...and of course, potpies. I was the only one of us boys that liked beef potpies and was ordered to mark the frozen tops with some sort of fork-poked emblem to distinguish them from the others... as if failing to do so would cause my brothers to eat a beef one by mistake. Apparently, the deep walnut color and chunks of BEEF, were not enough to discern a difference with a layman's eye. I actually enjoyed etching the hard pastry. It was art.

We would take our once frozen, now hot, dinners and sprawl out across the shag carpet in front of the black and white, 13-inch television. My mother had elevated the dining experience by purchasing two dinner trays in the shape of cows. My memory only recalls two cows so, I can surmise Johnny was still highchair bound. I recall with great clarity one was green and the other orange, and my cow was the green cow. However, when we moved later that year, and whilst unpacking the cows for our first dinner in the new home, we discovered the orange cow had broken off one of his horns.

I wasn't sure if using the term *cow* when referring to a male was correct, but Wiki-answers let me off the hook with the summation that though incorrect, it has become commonplace to do so. The correct term to use, as per Wiki, when not sure of the sex of the animal was "Cattle-beast." There was a word I had never seen before; sounded like something He-man might ride.

Immediately, my brother Brad commented on how sad he was my cow was now damaged. What!? My cow? I must have caused more head trauma than I thought with my day-before-the-move booby-trap as he was clearly not in his right mind.

The aforementioned *trap* was one of those moments where everything worked perfectly even though I didn't think it would and clearly hadn't contemplated the consequences. Like that time I threw a pencil at a teacher, never really anticipating it would actually make contact, and it stuck in his forehead, dangling like a cigarette off a dry bottom lip. Though, after the Principal's paddling I would venture to say it did *not* work out perfectly.

We were packing up for our move to Missouri and I was going through all of my toys…thinning the herd, if you will. I had compiled a box of assorted objects that I had either out-grown or destroyed so badly they were unsalvageable. In, said box, was a stack of hard plastic road strips one could snap together to create a race track.

At this point so many were missing the best I could construct was a misshapen semi-circle, trapezoid, parallelogram, cone…at best. Plus, I couldn't remember which cars were supposed to go with it. I am sure they're strewn in a million parts from Mississippi to Minnesota. Looking at that stack, I had a plan. I wasn't really thinking about consequences. I was more intrigued by the construction process than the end result, which of course, was to hit my brother in the head with the full load of unwanted toys. The contraption's blueprint is no longer in the forefront of my memory, but I have a faint recollection of a jump rope, duct tape, and the box of toys. Okay, not the most complicated engineering feat, but at the time I was the young age of…who knows? I know it predates *MacGyver* by about a decade and though no paperclip was involved, still a pioneering effort.

My room was on the second floor and to come up the stairs you first had to open a door. This is where I decided to establish the ambush. Teetering the overburdened box on the ledge at the top of the stairs, I attached the jump rope via duct tape to both the box and the door handle below. I then yelled for Brad, *I had something cool for him to see.*

This was a fool-proof phrase used by all kids to assure compliance. What person doesn't want to see something *cool*? My wife uses it on me time and time again to get me off the couch to look at something on Pinterest.

I sat in anticipation as I witness the turning of the knob. I was actually giddy to see if this would work.

Being the simple machine it was, it worked beautifully. He opened the door, the box fell spilling its enormous content onto the crown of his head with a satisfying *crack* of hard plastic to skull...beautiful. Within a blink, I realized what I had done. Blood was already seeping between his fingers, now pressed hard against what I would guess was a substantial gash. He wasn't crying at first...then he pulled his hands from his head and saw they were painted red...and it began. A slow wail, impressive enough to make an Irish keener jealous. I was struck by two things and not in the way Brad was struck...one was, he was over-reacting and two...I was in deep trouble.

Though my brother was a tiny waif and I a large tub of goo...at this point in my life he held the older brother intimidation factor and I was afraid of him. I immediately slammed my door and locked it with the impenetrable hook and loop assembly. You ever wonder what this type of lock was supposed to stop? The screw-in portion was fine-threaded and only a half inch long. A motivated box turtle could push his way through. But, like a blanket over your head protects your from monsters, the door was a barrier in which I had confidence to keep an enraged, bloody brother out.

My brother did not come up, but rather ran outdoors to Mom who took a look, and in good ol' Weilert fashion, decided a doctor was not necessary. She cleaned it and Super-Glued it shut. If it could suspend a grown man by a hard hat, surly it could keep his brains from oozing out. While this was going on, I removed the jump rope and made my way to the make-shift ER at the kitchen sink. Here is the thing, no one suspected me of anything. They both thought that somehow at the exact moment he opened the door, a box I was packing for the move decided to fall. As unbelievable as that was, I just don't think either of them could mentally grasp that I would do such a horrific thing to my sibling and as a result the subject was never broached.

So, it is this head injury that leads me back to my brother not being in his right mind when misidentifying the *green* cow as his own. I started to launch into a defense of my claim to the plastic bovine, but when I weighed the horrific atrocity I had waged against him just days before…my guilt got the better of me and I, from that point on, was the proud owner of a one-horned, orange Cattle-beast.

But, like I said, the family meals drastically changed at times my father was home. My mom transformed from, "Your TV dinners are in the oven," to Julia Childs without the annoying accompanying voice. It was during these times I migrated to her side. Though my mom could cook many things, my memory of her repertoire could be reduced to just four staples. Roast (every Sunday because my dad liked it), fried chicken (which I could never duplicate the taste), lasagna (it was just plain delicious), and porcupine meatballs (which contain no porcupine). Mom's meatballs became a much-sought-after delicacy at any pot-luck gathering. If you weren't in the first wave of diners, you would be left wanting.

Since I was the sole child who watched her create this one of a kind meal, I am the only one of my three siblings who can make it. My third sibling, yet to be mentioned, is my sister Michaela. She is twelve years my junior and was still a little kid when I left home. Michaela often feels as if she's an outlier on a stem-and-leaf plot. It was if she was part of our family, but experienced a childhood that was not; a single child raised by older, wiser parents who never relocated. I love her dearly and did not want her feel as though she was forgotten; but she literally didn't exist during most of times of which I write.

Now, every holiday where our family comes together, I am asked to *please* make the meatballs. When we eat them, it is as if we are all sharing a collective moment with Mom; a therapeutic ball of meat, which in no way sounds appetizing. It brings me great joy to be able to do this for my family. We all miss her greatly.

Now, like my mother, I too bring them to every pot-luck meal in which I am invited. Sadly, they are served in the same beat-up pot my mother cooked them in and it looks like something a hobo might use over open flames to heat up squirrel stew beneath an underpass, but it is just too sentimental to cast away. And, to be honest, the meatballs themselves really don't look spectacular. They get there name from the bits of rice that stick out from their sides looking somewhat like miniature-maggot-quills one might find on a porcupine from a Stephen King novel.

So, when given the options of safer choices like *Kentucky Fried Chicken*, which sort of violates the spirit of a pot-luck, and pasta dishes, I am often left with several meatballs to take home. It saddens me a bit as I know how awesome they taste. When people reject them based on appearance it is as if they are slighting my mom. I do understand, the best steak served on a trashcan lid just isn't appetizing. But, I will drag a thousand meatballs home, before I change the pot in which they are prepared. Plus, I have leftovers for days.

My wife does not eat leftovers…so she says. I am not sure what type of childhood she had where this was even an option. Either her mother was a wiz at calculating the exact amount of food her family would consume each meal, or she threw it away…something I could not see a frugal Greek woman doing; so my calculations tell me, my wife is lying. What she is really saying is, she doesn't eat MY leftovers. But, the lie, was in an effort to be nice. I truly believe in order for marriages to survive, one must be able to stretch the truth from time-to-time as an act of love to spare the feelings of one's spouse. And that spouse must accept the lie as truth even though, deep down they know it is cattle-beast feces.

Leftovers were a staple of the family diet. Usually, supper was the lone-cooked meal when we were growing up. Supper time varied in time, but we would usually be given a ten minute head's-up as to when it would make its appearance. And that time was non-negotiable. As my mom was so fond of saying, "We wait on each other like one pig waits on another." So, if you were late, you might just miss out on the meal. We were not a family that spoke as we ate. It was all business. Mom would make enough for Dad to take in his lunch box the next day and feed us as well. Dad always came first. I was an adult before I knew a chicken had white meat as the breast was always his when it came time to divvy up the pieces.

Our days would start with a breakfast of cereal. I remember *Quisp, Count Chocula* and *Peanut Butter*

Captain Crunch. Not the actual name brand products, but the ones with similar shapes and tastes that reside on the bottom shelf in large, sparsely marked bags. A line from a play I once read aptly put it, "They may look like Cheerios...but, SURPRISE; they're really Shitty-O's." Well said. But, no matter the manufacturer, all were sugar laden delights that left a film at the roof of your mouth.

During the summer, lunch was: come and graze at your leisure, or eat whatever you can find, or Mom's last resort line of, "Can't you go to a friend's house and eat...I bet they have better food?" We were busy kids in the hot days of June and July. There were bikes to ride; *The classic long frames with banana seats with playing cards clothes-pinned to the spokes making them purr as we cruised the streets. We'd use rocks to scratch white lines in the road to mark the distance of the longest wheelies...* nunchucks to make; *We were big into KungFu and made them using sawed off broom handles and pipes. We would tie them together using the stringer from our tackle boxes; more than once returning home with a goose egg on our forehead or in post self-wracked pain; hazards of learning the ancient art with only David Carradine as our master...* lifeguards to ogle at the pool; *We would splash each other until we got in trouble and had to stand in a circle right next to them...making sexual faces and thrusting our pelvises toward them when they weren't looking for the benefit of our friends, though at that point we knew nothing of what screwing might actually look like...* baseball games; *We loved baseball and would get games together with neighborhood kids and play in an empty lot until it got so dark someone took a ball to the face...* dirt clods to heave; *Although it was usually my brother and his friends throwing them at me. We would walk opposite sides of a hedgerow and throw them over the top at one another.*

*They were older and could make the toss creating havoc for
me as a tried to dodge the incoming bombs whilst trying to
locate suitable clods to return the favor. I remember
struggling to even clear the trees. It was a classic
mismatch...the full brunt of the US military vs...I don't
know... Rhode Island Cub Scout Troop 47...* BB guns to
shoot; *At beautiful birds we thought were so awesome we
killed them so we could see how they looked up close,
though at some point I quit doing this. Even at that age I
realized the troubling irony of our behavior. Mostly we
shot BBs at each other; wearing two or three shirts with the
stipulations of only one pump on the Daisy air rifle and
nothing above the neck counts. As if losing an eye would
be okay as technically you were still in the game. A
precursor to paintball, we were just ahead of our
time...*firecrackers to light; *We would blow up
anything...ant hills...plastic toys... It was nothing to see a
GI Joe with a missing hand because he foolishly didn't
throw the grenade in time. We also, and I write this with
some shame, would let toads eat Blackcats with a lit fuses
and watch them explode. I don't remember doing it often,
but once is really enough to burden guilt. In my defense it
did not escalate and I am proud to announce I am not a
serial killer...however, I wish I could be so sure of an older
neighbor boy just a few houses down. Sure, we were sick
little bastards, but he exacerbated, pause for giggle, the
torture, taking it a step too far. I don't know what this
guy's problem was with toads, but he had it in for them.
Maybe Mr. Toad went a courtin' with his mom...but he was
hell-bent on getting even. One day he called me to his back
yard to see something cool; I was powerless to resist.
When I rounded the corner I was horrified. He had used
fishing line to tie a toad spread-eagled to four sticks stuck
into the ground, belly up. In his hand he held a longer stick
with another strand of fishing line secured. I stood as if
watching a car wreck, I knew I should look away, try to*

protect my innocence, but I just couldn't. I had to see what was next. He then proceeded to take the make-shift whip and lash the soft underside of his victim. The skin peeled open with each swing.

"Cool, right?" was his comment.

I didn't want him to think I was a pussy, so I answered back, "Yeah, cool."

It was NOT cool! Two other times I fell for the magic phrase and each time it involved toads. The first, he had collected maybe five or six of the poor creatures and had hurled them onto a thorny locust tree, impaling them in various grotesque poses as if he were some artist of the absurd. The second, he had adhered a large muddy clod to the hind leg of the captive and threw him into a puddle just deep enough to where if he struggled greatly, he could just keep his nose above water. After witnessing such things, I never harmed another toad. As for him, I can't remember his name, but would not be surprised if it were Gacy or Bundy.

So, with all these things going on, lunch could never be a planned event. We ate when we were hungry. My mom, bless her capital of South Korea, had a habit of assuming with so many boys in the house, that food in the fridge would be eaten before it went bad. As a result, her efforts when it came to cleaning out the refrigerator were non-existent. In my life, my family rarely went to the doctor. We just didn't get sick with the occasional bug that might be going around. I attribute it to this fact; we ate things so vile over the years we created anti-bodies to all known diseases. I actually have a memory of cutting away some green-colored meat from the edges of a piece of bologna before slapping it on a mustard soaked slice of bread.

I cannot count the number of times, after we would eat heartily from the leftovers; my mom would enter the kitchen to proclaim, "Oh my, you didn't eat that did you? That's been in there forever."

To this day I use the, *does it taste too rancid to eat* method when determining if it is time to throw out any assortment of food product. This is bone of contention in my family who like to go strictly by the expiration dates. My claims that, those arbitrary markings are just there to get us to prematurely buy a replacement to feed the capitalistic market, are rejected by my wife and kids. I often times find myself having to hide food in the back of the refrigerator to protect not only the food, but my way of life. But, too often, like my mother, I forget about them and they start donning moldy-fuzz-winter-coats to protect themselves from the chill.

And the capital of South Korea is Seoul. In case you missed the pathetic attempt for clever word play.

10

The Fifth Encounter

It was Mother's Day…1:00 am and I was in the kitchen on a stool thinking about mom. I sometimes go months without even really thinking on the matter of having a deceased parent and then *BAM,* it hits me. I hadn't been to my mom's grave since the funeral. I just never wanted to experience whatever emotions I would experience if I went back. I have a hard time purposefully putting myself in a position where I know I will be miserable. Others may find comfort in actions such as these and that is great…but I just never wanted to run the risk. I know my brothers, sister and father have returned to tidy up and put down flowers, but not me. From the outside I may seem to be selfish, and maybe I am. I just don't see the point in talking to my Mom's ashes. Also, I am pretty sure the city hires people to keep the cemetery nicely mowed and tidy. The whole parade or *charade* is for the living not the dead and this living guy just doesn't see the need.

The mouse appeared across the kitchen atop the stove. She crouched amongst a gathering of items that should have be put away; remnants of a pancake breakfast. Left out was the frying pan, which really doesn't get that dirty if you cook them right, a spatula, a batter bowl coated with a now dry, caked paste that will be a pain to clean, and a half-empty bottle of off-brand, lite maple syrup, a misplaced calorie reduction in an effort to maintain my girlish figure. My wife hates that I buy it. I really think they just take regular syrup and add water. The shit is just runny. My wife, who comes from New York and had syrup trees on her family's property, was used to the *real* stuff; thick, dark maple and molasses.

Leading up to the funeral, our extended family gathered at the family house. A log home built by my father on a ten acre plot of land just outside of the town we finally settled in once my father made a commitment to my mom to stop traveling. He went through a series of jobs before landing a position at a cement plant as a mechanic. It was a huge reduction in pay, but a promise is a promise and he socked away his pride and stayed put. As I mentioned, we were a frugal family and so when it came time to acquire a vault to protect my mother's urn beneath the soil in the cemetery, rather than purchase one, my dad went down to the cement plant and poured one.

As we sat around eating the many assortment of sympathy food brought by my mom's many friends, I became bored and asked my father if there was something I could do. He stated he wanted the vault covered with tar to help it not leak. I thought back to the words of the funeral director in New York as he referenced the worms. Though I would doubt there would be much interest in ashes, I couldn't shake the thought. So, I accepted the task. He stated there was a five-gallon bucket just inside the garage door to complete the job.

The mouse rose up and started to lick her front paws. I guess as a result of having stepped in misplaced droplets of the syrup's sugary goodness. I could tell by her face she had no idea of the calories I was saving her.

Once in the garage, I located a large stiff brush and the bucket just inside the door as my father had described. I made my way to the vault, which sat on a trailer hooked to his truck, ready for the two hour trip to my mom's hometown later that day. I pried the top off the bucket. The sticky substance was thick and dark and I was already regretting not changing clothes. As I dipped the brush in and smeared my first stroke...I had this thought something wasn't right. Perhaps, I should have stopped and asked my dad, but I didn't. I pushed the thought aside and continued. After I had completely covered the vault, the layer looked too thin to get the job done so I lovingly applied a second coat. Worms had no chance. With the much needed two-hour distraction completed, I hosed-off and returned to the house. Though proud I could do this laborious task for my mom, in the back of my mind I still had that feeling something wasn't just quite right.

With paws cleaned the mouse leapt from the stove top to the floor and slowly walked in my direction. She disappeared out of sight for a moment on the far side of the island bar where I was seated. I heard the frantic scratch of small claws as she somehow scaled the side of the bar to reappear opposite me. It was then I crossed the line. I gazed straight in her eyes and asked, "Mom?" Look, I know the damn mouse isn't my mom...really. But, it was Mother's day, I was thinking about her a lot lately and here was this rodent right in front of me time and time again. Plus, she showed up, this for the fourth time, minus my dream, immediately following my insane thoughts on the matter. I wanted her to be my mom. I wanted to believe she was still out there somehow checking up on me.

Once inside the house I went to my father and told him I had finished, but something wasn't right. I asked if he would come out and take a look. He followed me to the trailer and immediately confirmed what I already knew. "Brian, you painted the whole thing with molasses!"

"Twice," I elaborated.

Somehow, right next to the tar was a bucket of molasses. Why? I don't know! In in all my years of being part of this family we had never purchased even as much as a thimble of the stuff. Who needs five gallons of molasses?! I immediately thought of the worms. My God, I had sent an invitation that would draw worms and other insects for miles. I was so embarrassed. My father, a man torn with sorrow did something I had not seen him do since the hospital. He laughed. He laughed so hard tears escaped the corners of his eyes. I laughed. What a gift of forgiveness he had just bestowed upon me. My mom who had a glorious sense of humor was indeed laughing too…I needed to believe that.

The mouse moved closer after I spoke. I dared not repeat it…Mom. I saw no harm on this night of suspending reality…of letting go of what is and is not possible. It was Mother's day after all and I felt I deserved a mother…even if it were a memory in the form of a mouse. She took another few steps and I leaned my head down to rest upon my hands on the bar. She took a few more steps and was now just inches from my nose. I could see her little whiskers twitching as she gauged the safety of the situation. I held firm and she closed the final gap.

My father's next duty, as per Weilert law, was to enter back into the house and humiliate me in front of the whole family. My two brothers always saw me as a bit of a screw-up; this would just reinforce their belief. But, I didn't mind. It was just who we were as a family and really it was such a colossal dumbass move, how could I begrudge anyone for poking a little fun. If the roles were reversed, I too would have partaken.

Our noses touched; her's was tiny, cold, moist and tickled me a bit as it wiggled up and down. My nose was thick and bulbous; a running joke with those who know me.

I have the nose of a black man. Now, before I am labeled racist, allow me to at least digress. This comment was issued by Walter Odell Green while I was in the Coast Guard. Walter is black. In fact not only did he state my nose was that of a black man, he insisted we measure the width of both his and mine to determine the greater girth. I won…if you want to call it that. I have great fears it will never stop increasing in size and it will be a large baked potato by the time I near retirement. My wife will leave me and I will die alone in want of companionship, sour cream and chives.

However, my brothers do not make fun of me. Johnny has my nose and Brad has my mom's nose. A nose-shape we referred to throughout the years as a butt-nose or penis-nose. Yes, my mom had a butt and or penis nose. She herself would admit it though I don't recall her using the actual words butt or penis. That was a gift we bestowed solely on Brad. What made their noses unique was the downward position with a crease in the center. In truth, it is a stretch to call it a penis, but it was fun to say, and really fun to say to Brad…penis-nose…try it. As to being insensitive to my deceased mother, I would just say to you, you just don't know our family.

So, there we were nose-to-nose. I didn't want to do anything to mess up this magical moment, but I couldn't help myself. Did I mention it was Mother's Day? I whispered, "I love you." Big mistake. It scared the shit out of her; literally. She simultaneously dumped two micro-turds and shot with such great speed in the other direction it was if I had lit her on fire. Within the blink of an eye she was gone from sight. Man, how I regretted my choice. I suppose if I had heard her whisper, *I love you*, I too would have reacted in kind. I remained still for a few moments and then started to cry. What a screw-up.

11

Scabby Nipples and Ass-Whoopin's

Our family summer vacations consisted of my mom
shopping for and then packing enough food to feed the
whole clan for several days of camping. Once at the
location she would then get to set up the camp and prepare
every meal. She got to wash dishes and sit around the
camp while we ran off playing and my dad fished. She did
all of this in the heat of July. I can think of nothing more
fondly than these trips and I am sure my mom felt the same
way.

These trips were often taken alone, but from time to time
with friends of the family or relatives. On one particular
trip, of which I will openly admit has some memory
glitches and could be a few of these very similar trips

combined, we were camping with: my mom's older brother, Uncle Pete, his wife, kids, a work friend of my father's, who I honestly remember being named Dick Skinner, and his daughters. I should point out I will not make fun of the name Dick Skinner as it is just too easy of a target and conjures up all sorts of visuals a normal person doesn't want to think on for any period of time. I should also point out I remember one of his daughters having enormous breasts. Now, I was young, maybe ten at the time, so the fact she slightly filled out a bikini top might cause a future memory of enormity…so I can't actually testify under oath, but I can say they made an impression.

On the day in question we were told of a giant tire swing suspended over a deep section of the creek near our campsite. We were all bored, looking for something to do, so we grabbed our inner-tubes and started to go. The tubes in use were black, rubber utility tubes; as capable of fixing a flat as they were suspending a child at the surface of the water. Mom pulled me aside and gave me a T-shirt to change into that was okay to get dirty and wet. Apparently, I was wearing a *nice* T-shirt at the time. To me they looked the same.

I always wore a shirt when I swam as the chunky fat that rippled at my sides and the pre-pubescent man-boobs were something my skeleton older brother liked to make fun of, especially when he had an audience. Compound that with the fact we were going to the swing with my two cousins, both who were physical clones of my bony brother, and the two Dick Skinner daughters, one of which had payloads that would excite any preteen, and there was no way in hell I was parading my physique in front of that horde.

One last bit of information I hesitate to include as it is a secret I have painstakingly tried to conceal my whole life, is that I have what my mom called inverted nipples. They are there, the nipples I mean, but instead of poking out, like skittish prairie dogs they pull themselves in, just below the surface. Now, on rare occasions they will make guest appearances, but not often. I have always been shameful in this physical fact about my body. They just look like two sad, hollow eyes reflecting my disappointment. I have grown to accept this defect as an adult; plus chest hair helps in hiding the holes. Mom was always great about it; trying to convince me it was more mainstreamed than it really was. I used to stare at other kid's chests at the pool, *don't judge me*, and in all the time I did so, I never found a fellow invert. So, I knew Mom was just being nice...but I wanted to believe. I imagined a whole island where everyone was fat and walked around proudly with shirts off advertising the fact their nipples had gone a-hiding.

Due to Mom's struggle with weight, she understood me like no one else in the family could. Mom was always counting calories. We never had anything other than diet soda in the house and to this day I think regular pop tastes sickly sweet. She, too, was a shirt-wearer when she swam; a kindred T-shirt cloaker, hiding her shame and disappointment. Mom wasn't always this way. I have seen photos of a voluptuous young woman who my father said was an incredible water skier. But, we kids took a toll on her body, not only by her having to tote us around for nine months, but the effort it took to raise us, many times alone. It's hard to want to plop in a Richard Simmons' *Sweatin' to the Oldies* VHS when you have been wrangling children all day.

Science tells us stress is one of biggest contributors to weight issues, and when it came to Mom's stress, I can't help but thinking I was the biggest contributor. At some point my Mom stopped spanking me. She had tried rolled up newspapers and coat hangers and still I stood defiant. Finally, she resorted to this terror-laden phrase, "You wait 'til your father gets home!" At first the utterance of those words yielded immediate results for her, but as she used them time and time again, like an overused drug, the affect began to wane as I built up immunity.

My dad would work out of town during the week and return on the weekends. So, if early in the week I had an infraction and knew I was already going to take an ass-whooping…I had nothing to lose the remaining days. When dad arrived, tired from a long week and drive, the first duty he had was to make good on Mom's promise. To say the least, my father and I had a strained relationship early on in my life. Now, as an adult, I can look back and have pity for the man; what a lousy situation to be put in. I am sure he would have rather kicked back, had a beer and enjoyed his family, which I know he missed dearly. Where other men would stay at hotels, my dad would drive three states home arriving early Saturday morning only to have to make the return trip on Sunday.

At first it was more bark than bite. Dad would fold his belt in half and hold it gripped between both hands. By pushing the leather together and then pulling it tight, it would make a satisfying *snap*; a sound that created instant fear of what was to come. Once in my room I would get a swat or two from his bare hands. But, these were not normal hands. These were the hands of a man who used them every day in hard labor. They were strong and calloused. These were hands I had seen bend steel and pick up red hot coals.

As I became more brazen in my behavior, the bark went away and the bite intensified as the belt was introduced into the main event. With each stroke, I would remain stoic. I knew all I had to do was cry and he would stop, but I would not give him the satisfaction. I took up the habit of hiding a magazine in my underwear to defray some of the pain. But, that was soon discovered.

When the belt failed, he tried to get creative by making my go to the back yard and chose my own willow switch with which to punish me. I learned to always select a thick one. It allowed for a solid consistent stroke that would land firmly on my bottom. The thin ones had a whipping action that created a stinging pain and were far less accurate...often times leading to misses that would land on the tender backs of my legs.

My punishments didn't always involve physical contact. Hell, hitting me did no good anyway. Sometimes, when I had pushed them a bit too far they would send me to my room. I have a memory that I later verified with my father that best illustrates just who I was as a child. One night when I was sent to my room I decided to scream bloody murder until they either came in to spank me, which I would have considered a victory, or released me which, of course, would be a point in my column. I am stubborn, but so were both of my parents. They had to be. I remember thinking to myself I was not going to stop screaming until I had some response. In the living room they must have reached a secret pact to die before they gave me the satisfaction of so much as a, "SHUT UP!" I screamed for hours upon hours at the top of my lungs. I remember being impressed I could keep it up that long. The exact time involved is not known, but I feel comfortable in claiming it started before dark and went on past midnight. My parents never budged; impressive. You hear of people who have the patience of Job…well Job would have entered my room and bludgeoned me to death to get some peace.

I am not sure how it all worked out over the years, but at some point the spanking grew less and less and eventually stopped. Maybe I grew up a bit. I like to think so anyway. I do not hold any feelings of ill-will toward either of my parents for if I had a child like myself; I would most likely be incarcerated for murder.

At camp, with my *play* T-shirt on, I was ready to go. We all walked to the spot and after a few double-dares and fear- facing we braved the swing. It would carry us far out to the center of the creek where we would let go; dropping deep into the muddy depths. When we eventually tired of climbing the steep incline to get to the rope, we settled into just swimming using our inner-tubes as resting points. I don't remember any specifics about that afternoon except I was made fun of for wearing a shirt and karma is a bitch.

As the day concluded and we returned to the camp a funny thing happened. Both Brad and my cousin started to complain that their nipples were sore. The rubber from the inner-tubes had stripped the outer skin as they repeatedly slid, chest first, into water and climbed back on, chest first; friction. As the chill of the night came, their perky little guys were so sore that both of the boys had trouble wearing shirts at all. By morning, their nipples were scabbed over. My little guys were tucked safely away and with the shirt as extra protection, free and clear of any damage.

I cannot know the pain they suffered, but to this day they speak of that fateful time on the tubes. Mom and I had many secret moments where we laughed about the whole situation. "Serves them right for making fun of you," she would say with that crooked grin; such is the irony of life.

12

The Sixth Encounter

For the first time, I awoke each night late for the sole purpose of a chance encounter with the mouse. Two weeks in a row I arose, walked to the kitchen and sat for an hour or two with no contact. If I am anything, I am tenacious.

I remember the first time I decided to actually turkey hunt on our father-son weekend. I so badly wanted to prove I could get one just like the others. If I didn't I just knew I would be ridiculed and I was not going to let that happen.

On the last day of the hunt, I went to one spot, at 6:00am… and sat. I sat there all day. I was a novice hunter and didn't have the fancy equipment of my dad and brothers, one of which is a butt pad. My ass was so sore, but I sat. Every now and again I would stand and get feeling back in my legs…or to go to the bathroom. I should note at this point another important lesson I learned on that day; make sure to bring toilet paper with you and never poop, upwind, close to where you are sitting. So, now braving my own stench as well, I sat. I played tic-tac-toe in the dirt with a stick and sat. I dug a small pit and put a red ant and a black ant in it to have a death match for my sick amusement…while I sat. I thought of how I would spend lottery money if I won, wrote a song in my head, cured cancer, solved world peace…all while I sat and sat and sat. I should mention that every so often I would pause and pull a few strokes on the box call my father had purchased for me…as I sat.

Morning turned to afternoon…to late afternoon…to early evening and still I sat. I talked with God and made a deal that if I sat here all day, if I was steadfast, he would reward me with a turkey. As the sun started to set and the woods grew dark and cold, I thought all my stubbornness was for not…then I heard it, a gobble; a tom turkey desperate for a mate. Like the single guy at the bar when *last call* is announced, he was running out of time. He was looking for a hen to bed down with for the night so he could get some early lovin' in the morning. I made one more sexy screech across the box call to coax him into thinking he was going to score. I couldn't see him yet but my legs were completely numb; I could not feel my feet at all and I knew there was no way I could shoot. I tried to stand, but my legs didn't want to cooperate. I pulled myself up and was finally able to balance against a tree. Due to the drop in temperature, my lack of food and water, and the adrenaline dump that comes with the nerves of hearing a mighty gobble in the woods, I couldn't even hold my gun as I was shaking too badly. It gobbled again and I hid behind the tree opposite of the direction of the noise. Then I heard the crumble of dry leaves made by the slow steady steps of a turkey. He was close. I picked up my gun and pulled it to my shoulder waiting for him to crest the hill. I tried to pick out a bush in the distance to see if I could steady myself enough to aim…it didn't look good. And then there he was, his head changing from brilliant red to intimidating white. He gobbled once more and I nearly peed myself. Hidden from behind, I again attempted to steady the gun, the whole time talking to God as if he had agreed to our little deal…"You promised…remember, you promised…"

I put him in my sights, it was nearly too dark to see and the shaking made a shot only approximate…I pulled the trigger. BOOM! It echoed through the timber and the tom turkey was on the ground flopping. It was as if I was in a Baptist tent revival and called up front as a cripple and the preacher touched my legs and screamed, "Healed!" as they were miraculously cured as I sprinted at him. As I drew close, he stopped flopping and regained his composure. He was sitting there, head up, and alert. I swung the butt of my gun around just as he turned his head to look at me. I could see right into his eyes. He had the look of a death row inmate right before the switch was to be pulled and had come to grips with his crime and what was about to transpire. The turkey looked peaceful. I couldn't help but later think God had sent that bird for me and the turkey knew he was to be sacrificed.

But, that was later. At this time, in the heat of the hunt, I yelled, "Lights Out!" and bashed his skull in with a satisfying thump. It was over. Nearly fourteen hours of sitting and I carried my trophy back to camp, triumphant. Thank God…really.

So, I would wake every night until the end of time if that is what it took to see my mouse.

As luck would have it, I did not have to wait quite that long. At the end of the second week she once again appeared. I kept telling myself, *tonight is the night*, and so, I wasn't surprised when I saw her. I was sitting at the kitchen table when she poked her head out from behind the cupboards. I smiled immediately and it was as if she reacted to this gesture coming toward me. I was hoping to be able to take this relationship further; to connect in some way that you only read about in fantasy novels and if you speak of them as if they are real, you get locked up in a rubber room.

However, I was torn as to whether to be bold and just see if there was any truth to any of my bizarre inner-thoughts. If it were meant to be then it was meant to be. But, this was tempered with the fear of what had happened at our previous interlude; me pushing the matter and her fleeing and disappearing for weeks. I missed her and didn't want it to happen again.

I remember hearing of a study designed to determine the future successes of children. The test claims to be more accurate in revealing a child's outcome than their upbringing, socio-economic status, ACT scores and other well-known factors. The study simply placed a marshmallow in front of the child and stated he or she could eat it now or wait and receive another one. They followed each of these children into adulthood and found ,nearly to a child, those who needed immediate gratification and ate only the first marshmallow, failed in life. Those who waited were all, by most standards, successful.

So, I decided to do nothing with the mouse; I would wait; perhaps there would be a second marshmallow on my horizon. She moved deliberately toward me, clawing her way up the chair on the other side, leaping on the table and closing the distance once again to less than a few inches from my face. I did nothing. She once again sniffed at my nose. I did nothing. It was time for the second marshmallow. My mouse, my mom the mouse, did something that so astonished me that I don't expect anyone to believe it. I wouldn't if I were told by someone else.

I had not let my wife in on any of my late night rendezvous. She hated mice. I was afraid she would set a trap or put out poison. Okay, I know she wouldn't set a trap. Setting one of those ranked higher on her fear scale than an army of mice. To be honest, I hate setting them too. I mean really, we have the internet and this is the best we can come up with? I am aware of the old saying *build a better mouse trap and you make a smarter mouse*, but come on; are we so afraid of a master-mind race of rodents taking over the world we stopped trying in the 1897? Ironically, I *Googled* it and found out James Atkinson patented the "Little Nipper" nearly a hundred and twenty years ago. They are mice people, not Sky Net!

If I were to all of a sudden tell my wife about what the mouse did…well, in spite of what she might say because she loves me and knows I miss my mom…she wouldn't believe me.

My mom, of this I am now convinced, rose on her hind feet and put her hands together in prayer. She looked me straight in my eyes and they weren't the eyes of a mouse, they were my mom's. She stood there staring at me. I felt I knew what she wanted. I pulled my hands together and when I did, she closed her eyes.

I didn't even know mice had eyelids. Maybe I knew, but I don't recall ever seeing one even blink. I too closed my eyes…well pretend closed them like you did when you were a kid and wanted your mom to think you were asleep on the couch so you could still watch late-night, monster movies on TV. I think mom always knew I was awake, but she really liked me, somehow, and I think with dad gone I was good company. She would just put a blanket over me and let me be. Besides, I was the only one with which she could watch scary movies. Johnny was too young and Brad ran to his room and pulled the door tight whenever he heard just the theme music from *Creature Feature*.

I grew up in the Catholic faith and so praying for me was very impersonal. As a kid the fact that I memorized the prayers was more important than the actual purpose or meaning of the prayers. Mass, with the exception of the five minutes the priest went off script, seemed to repeat itself year after year. Seen one Catholic Christmas mass? You've seen them all. As an adult I can take a different take on it, but as a kid I was more worried about messing up when to stand and sit and kneel and what to say at the right time and should I go to communion if I am thinking about cartoons and not God and how long before we eat roast when we get home. What I am saying is that praying, really praying from the heart, is tough for me.

Recently, I had visitors come to the door and hand me a flyer. They claimed it covered the six most asked questions about the bible and God. I guess I can pray a little bit as the whole time I am listening to them, I am praying they don't ask to come inside; one was an old dude and I didn't want to be rude. My prayer must have been answered as they thanked me when I accepted the paper and went away.

As I read through it, I was curious as to what they thought were my six top questions, I came to question number three, "Does God hear our Prayers?" I am not sure what church they were affiliated with as it was nowhere to be seen on the flyer, but I think they may be anti-Catholic. I am paraphrasing of course, but the gist of how number three was answered is God doesn't like scripted repetitive prayers. It hints of the prayers needing to be unique and personable. I found this troubling. It concerns me that I need to be some sort of slam poet before God will take notice of me. Plus, the *Lord's Prayer* and *Hail Mary* are classics. As a teacher I hate to see the classics ignored.

I will just come out with it; the mouse's lips were moving. Again, I wasn't even sure mice had lips, or had given it a thought, but even through squinty eyes, at five inches; I am clear on what I saw. I should have been praying too as this was clearly some sort of miracle, but at that point God was the furthest thing from my mind. I whispered, "Mom?" She opened her eyes and stared at me. She looked disappointed in my lack of participation. I knew that look all too well. I dropped my hands and put them flat, palms up, on the table. She dropped to all fours, reached out and put her right hand on the finger tip of my pinky finger. I began to tear up and her eyes softened. There was love in them, but something else. It was as if they had a longing, a sorrow in them as well. A drop fell from my cheek and lit squarely in the center of her forehead. She didn't flinch. "Mom," I stated; this time not a question. And it was if that gave her permission to leave. She turned and moved away, and I will never be the same again.

Damn Yankees

I figured out the other day that my wife and I have lived in fourteen houses in our twenty-five year marriage. I was repeating the sins of my parents. I just get restless and feel it is time to move on. Maybe this is a remnant of my childhood. Much of my time as a kid is a blur. I vaguely remember only two schools and just a handful of friends. The towns and people just merge into one big glob of memories. It is hard to discern a small town in Indiana from one in Missouri or Illinois or Kansas. The only blaring culture shock was the move from Minnesota to Mississippi.

We had lived in Minnesota for just one year. But, that was long enough for my parents to create another human being, Johnny. Maybe he was created in Indiana or Missouri…or

wherever we lived prior to Minnesota, but he was born in
Minnesota. My memories from that year in the far north
are limited to just a few. I recall a massive storm that left
snow piled up so high, we couldn't get out the front door.
When we finally did, Brad and I, wearing our snowmobile
suits, tunneled the entire length of the yard to emerge at the
mailbox. Mom stayed inside, most likely watching *As the
World Turns*...no fear of a four and six year old being
buried alive under hundreds of pounds of snow...after all I
was atop my YMCA preschool due to the fact I knew the
alphabet forward and backwards. Brad, though not the best
student, could make things with his hands like paper
airplanes and rubber band slingshots. Sure, Brad and I
were a ways off from earning our engineering degrees, but
by my mom standards, we had it covered. Plus, more
important things were going on inside the house like:
*Michael Shea was planning to claim Lisa Shea was an unfit
mother to Chuckie and he was going to blackmail her, but
before he could he was shot and killed. Tom Hughes was
put on trial for the crime and convicted, but it was actually
Miss Thompson who killed Michael.*

I loved the Darwin approach to parenting in the late 60's
and early 70's. Where today teeter totters and monkey bars
have been removed from playgrounds due to fear of injury
and lawsuits, in that time, it was nothing to see a kid
younger than ten mowing a steep, inclined yard barefoot.
Though I know it isn't true, it was as if parents back then
figured if you were too stupid to survive...you probably
shouldn't. I know I shouldn't say it, but as a teacher, every
year I teach a few students that evolution would have
weeded out a long time ago had they grew up in that era.
It wasn't just my parents who embraced this philosophy; it
was mainstreamed. At the YMCA were I attended
preschool, they also had swimming lessons. My mom

decided to take both Brad and I for a week long class. I should point out I could hold my breath longer than most and took to the water as if I were a tadpole. I loved swimming lessons. My love of water continued on into adulthood as I was the rescue swimmer on my Coast Guard cutter. However, Brad's experience was one of a different nature. Brad struggled to stay afloat even with the aid of water wings. He was terrified. But, rather than being sympathetic to a six-year-old's fear, they took a large shepherds hook and kept pushing him to the center of the pool each time he tried to reach the side; some tough love. Brad did this for two days before telling me he had had enough. When mom dropped us off each morning, Brad would go and hide for the one hour class. When Mom came to pick us up, she was none the wiser. I promised Brad, who was my best friend, I would keep his secret, but it only lasted until the final day of lessons when the YMCA had a little assembly to hand out completion certificates and Brad didn't get one. My mom inquired as to why and discovered he had stopped going to class... Not sure what happened to Brad on that one, but he may have earned some lenience due to the aggressive actions of the swim staff.

The journey to Mississippi had an ominous start. My dad, ever the penny-pincher, decided rather than just throwing money down the drain by renting a U-Haul, he would opt to buy an old truck that wasn't running...fix it...use it for the trip...and then sell it once we were down south. After weeks in the driveway, he finally got it running. Its maiden voyage was short lived for as he put it in reverse he heard a loud crunch within a few rolls of the tires. My dad had backed the giant truck over my most favorite childhood toy of all time, Marvel the Mustang. He felt horrible as he knew what it meant to me and tried to comfort me with,

"Serves you right for leaving it in the driveway." Sounds harsh, I know, but what he said didn't match the look on his face or the way he said it. It was as if he was forced to recite some old script passed down by his father. But, he was saddened by doing it...I just knew.

What made Marvel *a marvel* was that you sat atop the horse and by bouncing up and down, it galloped down the road. It was the most liberating feeling of freedom for a four year old. And of course my mom let me ride it down the middle of the street. Again, I'm sure she figured if I were too dumb to get out of the way of an oncoming car, what were my odds of survival anyway? This loss devastated me. It was my first memory of dealing with death.

That was the beginning of our trip south. Dad drove down alone while Mom loaded Brad, baby Johnny and I into a packed car. I know from later conversations as an adult, the truck broke down several times on the way. We made the trip without any major incidences until we crossed the border into the state of Mississippi. We had the typical minor issues along the way...where Brad's feet would cross the invisible center line on to my side of the back seat. I had to immediately establish that I was willing to protect my homeland lest he be encouraged into manifest destiny. So, I karate chopped his foot. Of course, as with all military conflicts where the more powerful army is attacked, whether they are in the right or not, he retaliated with a mule-kick. Johnny, who was not quite one, was safe in the front secured in his car seat; enough distance to avoid taking any collateral damage. Though to be honest, I am guessing there really wasn't a car seat.

As the conflict ensued, my mom was forced take on the persona of my dad; she, his understudy in the role of vehicular disciplinarian. Phase one was the threat of, "Don't make me pull this car over," delivered while feinting a backhand slap and staring at us intently in the rearview mirror. When that failed, she moved into phase two which was to pump the brake like she was going to pull over...depending on the severity of the situation this might also be accompanied with a slight steering swerve and an additional warning of, "I'm not joking!" Phase three, which was what we reached on the trip to our new home, was to actually start blindly swinging while trying to stay on the road. Maybe Johnny wasn't as safe as he thought; a possible innocent casualty of war.

There were three or more phases in the threat continuum: Four, pull car over, get out and come around to the back seat and swat at us. Five, actually pull us from the car and swat us publically along the roadside. Six, murder. Luckily, though close on many occasions, we never got to six.

That was the minor incident...the major one was we somehow got lost on a gravel road in the back country of Mississippi, which in and of itself is haunting, but then as if it were a scene out of one of those soft porn, college-age slasher movies, minus hot girls and athletic men with abs, our car just died. There were no payphones around and Dad had the CB with him, so that eliminated any chance of getting help from a *good buddy*.

Finally, after baking in the sun for some time without a single car passing by, Mom made the decision to walk to a country home she had seen a mile or so back. She rolled the windows up, leaving just a small crack, locked the doors, and told us to stay in the car and watch Johnny. She was alone and I am sure afraid, but she made a command decision, bucked it up, and started her trek. What else was she supposed to do? She was in a foreign land and was not quite sure what would open the door to the house she had to visit. I guessed she reasoned it was better to leave us on the roadside locked in a car than to hand deliver her whole family to cast of *The Hills Have Eyes*. An hour later she returned to the car with a squat black woman with a head of grey curls. She had brought us water. I am sure she said something nice to us, but that was overshadowed by the memory of being able to momentarily get out of the car to escape the July sauna. The woman said she would wait with us until a car came by. She told my mom that if, "They were white folk, you can flag them down and if they are black folk, I'll do the flaggin'."

As it happened, a white couple came by and took us to town. As I think back on the story, I don't think they gave her a ride home. But, maybe she didn't want one. Eventually, we got a hold of dad, the car got fixed and we made our way to our final destination, Staunton Drive in Southaven, Mississippi; a suburb of Memphis, Tennessee.

Now to understand what we stepped into you have to understand the dynamics of what I was told in regards to the naming of this Memphis suburb. If I am wrong, I apologize, but my experiences lean toward this being the truth. Southaven was apparently created in an effort to move north so as to create a white only community. It was called Southaven because, though it was the very northern border of Mississippi, it was a southern fringe of Memphis.

The word *haven* of course reflects a safe place. Get it; a safe place for white people. This story may seem flimsy until you hear that when Southaven became a bit more multicultural, a new affluent suburb to the north was established with the name of Whitehaven. I will let you break that one apart. It was the early 1970's and coming from the north Brad and I had no idea of what prejudice even was...we quickly learned.

The day after we arrived, my mom told me I should go ride my bike down the street and try to make some new friends. I made it about a block before a bunch of kids jumped me and knocked me from my bike. They were throwing punches and kicking me; the whole time calling me a, *damned Yankee.* I didn't know what that meant. They threw my bike into a bush and ran off laughing. Later that day, Brad went down and got my bike for me. I remember kids following him back and spouting off about *the South rising again* and we should go back to where we came. All I can guess is our Minnesota license plate gave us away and they were just parroting behaviors I am sure were modeled by the adults in their homes.

One of the boys came into the yard. I remember Mom was watching on the front porch as Brad went into attack mode. Like I said, he was little, but he was also scrappy. Housed within that tiny body was a future high school wrestling state champion. Within a split second, Brad had him on the ground and lit into that boy with a barrage of punches. I am sure he didn't expect that explosion from such a miniature stick of dynamite. Mom watched from the porch and didn't say a word. One of her children had been hurt and justice was being delivered. I can't say for sure, but I bet she was smiling.

After that, we magically had respect from the neighbor kids who eventually became our playmates. Plus, why hate on the northern, white people when there were so many black people to hate. Now, I am going to use a taboo word so often you might think you are listening to a Busta Rhymes CD. The word is *nigger*. I am telling you it was like they never made it past the Civil War. It was *nigger* this and *nigger* that when talking about black people. Even when they weren't trying to be racist they were subtly racist….ringing the doorbell and running away was called *nigger-knocking*…Brazil nuts were called *nigger-toes*…big rocks buried in the ground were called *nigger-heads*…fixing something cheap and on the fly was called *nigger-rigging*.

I don't recall how I handled the situation, but I have a memory of just being uncomfortable. In fairness, I should point out it was a two way street of hatred. I don't have many school memories, and this one is also a bit fuzzy, but I remember befriending a large white kid named Fred who clearly was held back a few years. I befriended him because the black kids at school wanted to beat me for not only being white but new as well. No one messed with Fred. For one year of my life I experienced much of what is bad in humanity. But, in spite of blatant bigotry, we *were* new and in need of friends. Kids aren't lucky enough to be so selective with whom they befriend. It is mainly an approximation formula. If you live close enough to ride your bike to their house and they are your age…Ta-Da, you are friends. Plus, on Staunton Drive, no one was what you would call rich.

Just down the road were the McGruder's, who let their little kids run around the neighborhood naked and covered in dirt. They had a boy named Jo Jo; a name we later stole in naming our poodle; a poodle that grew old and grey and mean as a rabid badger. Jo Jo and my dad had a love-hate relationship. Jo Jo would spend most of the time angry at the world and hiding under my mom and dad's bed. I remember my father trying to get the dog out from beneath and hearing Jo Jo go mad. My dad would get a broom and poke the handle at the dog until it latched on like a snapping turtle and my dad could drag him out. On the flip side that sick dog loved to lick my dad's toes. My dad would come home from a long day of work and pull off his boots and socks and Jo Jo would go to work. It was disgusting to watch, but both the dog and my dad seemed to enjoy it so who was I to judge? Also, it was most likely this disgusting duty performed by Jo Jo that kept him from going to the pound.

So, it was with the likes of Jo Jo McGruder and others I befriended… kids who, most likely, grew to be men with whom I would never associate; I'll own that. Once friends, we could laugh about our differences. They used to bust on Brad and I because we said *pop* when referring to a soda. When we asked for a *pop* they would just reply, "Your dad's not here." They called everything coke….If you asked for a Coke they would say, "What kind of coke? A Pepsi coke…a Mountain Dew coke…?"

We formed a football team called the Staunton Stompers and would go to other neighborhoods to take on their teams. Our front yard was the stadium for the Stomper's home games because we didn't have any real grass to tear up and our house was a rental.
I think Mom had it rougher than we kids. As an adult you have a harder time making friends due to the fact, you

know when someone is an ass and you don't want to be around them...something kids are oblivious to. Mom wasn't working and so this even further limited her in friend-making opportunities. As an adult, I can think back now and realize just how lonely my mom must have been with each of these moves. Kids are resilient in their ability to make friends, but my mom was not a kid. She was a very loving woman who had a gift for making others feel as though they were special...but the truth was I think she was very closed with her feelings...she had to be. In the ten years since I was born she had lived in ten different places; hard to establish deep meaningful relationships in such short spurts. This only made Mom cling closer to the things most permanent in her life; her family.

14

The Seventh Encounter

I slept through the night for the next four days straight. I never do this and suspected my wife was slipping me Ambien. She had been commenting on just how horrible I looked this past month…The words *raccoon eyes* were used on more than one occasion. But, she swears she hasn't been drugging me. I think for legal purposes she would lie even if she was. She wants to know why I seem so angry anyway; about sleeping …that I should be happy about it…Something's not right…she wants to know what's going on…she knows before my four-day crash I had been getting up a lot at night…even more than usual…

I wanted so badly to tell her, but I just couldn't. My wife is my best friend and confidant, but there is no way she could fathom what I was experiencing. Think about how this sounds, "Yeah, I have been getting up and spending time with a mouse…we prayed together the last time. Oh yeah, did I mention, she's my Mom?" You see my point. So, I lied, a little. I told her I had been thinking about Mom lately and it just seemed to hit me at night when I had down time. I am sure she didn't believe me, but she gave me a pass and for that, I was thankful.

I wonder what the mouse does when she's not around me? I start thinking during that time she is probably just an ordinary mouse doing…mouse things; eating at the insulation in the walls, pooping and peeing in my cupboards, scrounging for food bits or chewing into boxes of Kraft Macaroni and Cheese. I also think, I like it better that way. I would hate to think of my mom just waiting around for me, forced to live the life of a rodent; though she could be patient.

I remember finally taking a stand against the injustices of childhood bondage and servitude and proclaimed I was running away from home. Mom reacted in a way that took me off guard. She was very good about it, making sure I had packed enough food and some underwear. I was very serious about my independence. Well, as serious as an eight year old can be. I believe she gave me some advice on surviving on my own and told me she would miss me, but she understood. It was not going down at all like I had anticipated. So, loaded down with my backpack and Six Million Dollar Man lunch box, I headed down the street. I couldn't believe she was letting me go! What was wrong with her?

I kept walking, glancing back from time to time to see if she was watching. She wasn't. Two or three blocks down the road I reached a crossroad; not in the literal sense though I suppose there was one, but a decision. I could keep walking, a man on his own or admit to myself I was a boy who needed his mother. I decided on the latter. I turned and headed back. But, I didn't want Mom to think I didn't have the *cojones* to make it on my own. In all fairness at that age they were tiny. To save face, I went around the back of the house and shoved myself behind the air conditioner unit.

It was morning when I left and I knew I had to wait until at least dark for her to know I was to be taken serious and for her to start worrying about me. As I sat there I drew pleasure in the fact she would think I had been abducted by some pervert. I played out in my head, her calling the police crying and proclaiming what a horrible mother she was. As lunch passed I poured myself some warm tomato soup from the Astronaut Steve Austin thermos. Mom had made it for me telling me it gets cold at night and it would keep me warm.

At this time, I sort of expected some sort of activity. We had a bell on the front door and I would be able to tell if anyone came or went...no one did. I started to think Mom was serious about me leaving. My whole thinking process changed from one of getting back at her to one of what I did so wrong to make her not want to have me around. I wanted to run into the house and say I was sorry, but I was so damn stubborn, I couldn't...wouldn't.

So, I remained even as the sun started to set and a chill hit the air. I pulled my peanut butter and jelly sandwich out and ate it, wishing I had saved the soup. The bell rang a few times and I had brief hope she did care, but then I would hear Brad or Johnny talking and I knew it wasn't Mom. Even my brothers didn't seem to care. I thought she would send Brad out to look for me, she didn't. The darkness was a perfect match for my emotions. I was cold and confused. Was I such a bad kid? I might have cried, but I don't have that as a memory. I can't tell you exactly how long into the night I sat, but at some point I gave in.

As I entered the backdoor I didn't know what to expect. Mom didn't rub it in she had won, but allowed me to keep my dignity. She simply asked if I was okay and she was very glad I decided to stay. That was it. Many years later she shared with me she could see me the whole time from the kitchen window. She really did care.

I guess my reasoning went: Mom entered into the mouse when she wanted to communicate with me and other than that, the mouse would just be a normal mouse. It made sense to me…as much as any of this did.

I told my wife I was going to sleep on the couch. I claimed it was because I didn't want to wake her up in case I couldn't sleep. The couch was okay to sleep on, but my younger son, though he would deny it, somehow broke a spring in the middle cushion rendering it just uncomfortable enough to assure I would toss and turn during the night; thus giving me the opportunity to be ready in case I had a visitor. I turned on the TV to ESPN and drifted off to sleep. But, it wasn't the spring that woke me, but a tickling at my feet. It started as a dream of being attacked by a bunch of crawling bugs but when I woke, I realized there really was something beneath the covers, mingling amongst my toes. I quickly kicked the blanket to the floor and sat upright. There was enough light emanating from a re-telecast of a soccer game to make out exactly what had caused the commotion; Mom.

She was as startled as I was with the sudden flurry of motion, but held her position which was directly where my feet had been a second ago. She's lucky in my stupor I didn't kick the living daylights out of her. "What are you doing!?" was the first thing out of my mouth. After no response, "I could have killed you!" was the second. Each time I tell about my encounters, I feel as though I must be as accurate as I can, but in my attempts to be so truthful, I realize it just sounds as if it is all made up. I am honest in saying these times with the mouse trouble me in a way. I feel as though I am teetering on the edge of sanity. I whole-heartily believe these encounters to be something out of this world, but real. However, I am also cognizant to the fact that even as I document this story no one will ever believe me as it can't be real.

I suppose this is the very foundation of all the various religions. A blind faith in knowing what is true even though others may easily poke holes in the story.

I have taught students who are Mormon, and though I am respectful of their beliefs, I just don't believe the foundation of the religion. Seems to be a bit of a mouse story to me, but here I sit talking to a rodent whom I know is in some way the spirit of my dead mother. Faith is a troublesome thing when you are worried about what others may think.

Mom approached me once again, scampering up the blanket only to stop short of my crotch. She looked up at me once again as if she wanted me to do something and that I should know exactly what it was...I didn't.

"What?" I asked hoping for some sort of hint. She paused for a moment and then proceeded to climb up the blanket and onto my shoulder. She turned a couple of lazy circles, lay down and closed her eyes... and went to sleep. I didn't dare move. I wasn't in the most comfortable of positions, but that didn't matter; there was no way I was going to disturb this moment.

As a child I am sure it is customary to crawl into your parents bed at least a couple of times while growing up. There are always those moments that warranted it: that loud clap of thunder, a nightmare, fear of the monster under the bed or in the closet...but I don't ever recall doing so. I was such an independent person it never occurred to me. I wonder how many times when my father was on the road she wished for one of her kids to come in and cuddle to keep her company. Maybe my brothers did...but not me. I was always so egocentric it never occurred to me she might have been fearful of storms or had nightmares...or just been lonely.

My wife, who like me, is also a teacher, taught alongside of a man who claimed he could talk with the deceased. He even spoke with my wife's mother once. He later went on to write a book which I read…and to be honest, it was pretty convincing. So, if souls can just be floating out there ready to talk with us…why not a mouse? It is troubling to think about things such as these as it opens up so many questions. Through all my Catholic catechisms, I don't recall addressing this issue. I guess I was more interested in figuring out how dinosaurs played into the whole picture because to a kid, dinosaurs are way more interesting than souls.

I sat there looking at her sleep. Watching her little rib cage rise and fall with each rapid breath. She looked peaceful. It was then I noticed the Sharpie marker on the coffee table and I had a thought. I figured with the billions of mice in existence there was the possibility of more than one sharing my residence. I wanted to make sure I had the same mouse.

I eased myself forward making sure to not disturb her and picked up the marker. I removed the cap and carefully lifted the very end of her tail and colored the tip black. Satisfied I would not lose her again; I closed my eyes, for real this time, and fell asleep in spite of my upright position. When I woke that morning, she was gone and my back hurt like hell.

Washington, Baseball and the Lifesaverman

My wife and I took a trip to Hannibal, Missouri for a summer jaunt. I wouldn't call it a vacation but more of a recall of a vacation. Growing up, my family didn't take a lot of traditional vacations together. By traditional, I am talking about heading to a fun place that might actually have a brochure printed in color. Hannibal was one of the few we did take. I am not sure why I remember the boyhood home of Mark Twain being fun, but I do. Along the way to Hannibal, my wife and I made a stop in Monroe City, which is not a city at all. Monroe City is where I spent the next-to-last stop of my whirlwind, adolescent travels. After Monroe, my dad made good on his promise to settle; ending up in Wamego, Kansas where he still lives.

I wanted to stop by this small town because I was old enough during the time I lived there to actually have solid memories. As I said earlier, so much of my life is made up of ghost memories that hover between fact and fiction; the purgatory of reality. The first order of business was to find the place we rented when we had lived there. I remember calling it the white elephant; a hulking structure painted a stark white. I later learned, when my wife and I couldn't find it and visited the local newspaper, that it used to be the town hospital and it was torn down a few years back. I got directions to the now empty lot and tried to mentally recreate the image from forty years ago.

I couldn't. It bothered me. I had made the trip to try and reconnect with an elusive childhood in some concrete manner and now the home I most remembered wasn't even there for me to verify those memories. Using the empty lot as a staging point, I tried to navigate the town in a historic cerebral reconstruction effort. I was able to locate my good friend Monte's house where we played bumper pool in the game room above his garage. From that point I was able to navigate to the Catholic school I had attended.

Other than my very first kiss of Wendy Recowski in kindergarten and being slapped for my efforts, my most vivid school memory of rejection comes from this Catholic school. The school was both taught and patrolled by nuns dressed as penguins. I *now* know it is a cliché but the first time you hear it from the mouth of a fourth grader you think you are dealing with a comedic genius. Upon reflection it doesn't seem as though the rejection should have been too devastating, but at the time it was. As always, we were the new kids and the drive to make a good impression was paramount. It is a lot of pressure to show up on the scene of established cliques and try to break in. Even though we would be packed up and gone in a year, failure to work oneself into the right group at the onset could lead to a year of misery.

The Christmas before, I had received a wood burning kit. I found at an early age I was more artistic than my classmates. While the faces they drew were concocted of round heads with misshapen, lopsided eyes on foreheads, check-mark noses and lipless semi-circle smiles, mine were just better. I could not only draw realistically, but could see light and shadows to enhance the depth of the picture. I would go to the library to look at books to help me get better. I don't say these things to brag, but to lay the groundwork of my defense for being labeled a cheater.

At the start of the school year there was a Social Studies fair. For my project I drew an awesome picture of our first president onto a piece of wood and then unleashed my new found wood burning skill set. I finished off George with acrylic paint that really brought out his eyes....which were not on his forehead. The night of the competition I walked around looking at the other projects and felt pretty darn secure I had locked down the purple ribbon. However, as the evening unfolded, and the colored pieces of fabric were awarded...I saw my work of art earned a lowly green participation award...and I use the word *award* with great disdain. This is not a case of sour grapes, but really, I'm telling you it wasn't even close. Mom told me to relax and she would find out what happened. She reminded me of the ass I had made of myself just a baseball season ago.

This is again going to sound as if I have the ego of…*insert someone you think has a huge ego*, but the truth of the matter; I was a really good baseball player. My forte was I could smack the dog crap out of the baseball. Not only had I grown tall, apparently, I had also figured out how to get my substantial fat moving in the right direction when it came to swinging a bat. It was nothing for me to hit two or three homeruns every game. So, at the end of the season, when we had our baseball picnic and they were giving out the *best hitter* award, I knew I was a lock. All the trophies up to that point, for the various other awards, were impressive in size. I was already trying to figure out where the monstrosity would be placed in my bedroom.

Finally, the last award, my award, was being announced and they did indeed call my name. As I approached the front, I immediately saw a huge problem. Where the other trophies were at least thirty-six inches in height, the trophy they were about to hand me was less than twelve. This was supposed to be the marquee award and I was to be given this…this bacteria-sized artifact of shame? While others clapped, I, in a stunned state of denial, took the token object in disgust and stomped back to my seat.

Then it started, this angry, crying, complaining tantrum in front of all of my friends and their families. I had been a kid the others looked up to strictly due to my skills on the diamond. But, I was about to end all of that. Without going into the details where I *might* have proclaimed, whilst screaming at the top of my lungs, I was better than all of the others put together, or Danny only won the best teammate award because he was the worst ballplayer in the history of the sport. In short, I made a complete ass of myself and my poor mother, who was always at my side during my baseball endeavors, could do nothing to stop my frenzy. At first she tried to save face looking the reasonable parent as she tried to talk me down under her breath. But, when it was clear I was having none of that, the best she could manage was to grab me by the arm and aggressively drag me to the car.

I wished I had stopped and listened to her because what she told me in the car stuck with me my whole life; a lesson hard learned. She told me one of the coaches had approached her before the awards and told her the trophy company had messed up and one of them was substantially smaller. He said they tried to think of what kid was mature enough to handle it and they thought of me. He asked my mom what she thought, and she assured him I was mature enough to handle it. So, the small trophy was the reward after all; the respect of the coaches…which I gave away in a moment after spending a season to earn it. I pass this lesson on to all the kids I coach. I tell them if they are motivated by plastic and metal trinkets, they are missing the point. The goal is to pursue personal excellence, whatever that might be for the individual, and gain the satisfaction that comes from the effort it takes to be at your best. If you do this, you will *happen* to win awards along the way…but if you don't, you will still have a sense of accomplishment no other person can give or more importantly, take away.

So, this time I waited for Mom to investigate what was going on in regards to the public slighting of Mr. Washington. Mom waited until we were secure in the car, alone, before telling me what she had uncovered. Apparently, at the baseball picnic, she too had learned a lesson. Simply put, they didn't believe I had done it alone.

They thought for it to be *that* good, my dad had to have helped me. What an outrage! How dare them!? Basically, without saying it, the inscribed *participation* ribbon they taped to my project should have had the word *CHEATER* on it instead …but on such short notice that must have been unable to locate one.

I was struck with the fact my mom didn't defend me. I am sure I asked her time and time again if she told them that, *I did do it.* I don't remember her even responding. She was very quiet as if she were ashamed. At the time, I didn't get it. *They* should be ashamed. Maybe it is just bad form to argue with a nun; not a habit to get into. Plus, she too was new and without friends. I bet she just wanted to disappear into the background without making a scene. It was bad I was starting the year known as a cheat, but kids would forgive me and I would make friends, but she was the mother not only of the cheater, but she knew about the offense and allowed me to enter. These were very damning character flaws other mothers and the clergy might not be so quick to forget. As I grew older, I understood just how many adults love to relish in the misery of others. I do want to mention on the behalf of my mother and myself, I did do the whole thing alone…except for this super cool eagle in the upper-right corner my dad drew…then wood-burned…and painstakingly painted.

I had developed into a loud kid. My guess is all the pressure to quickly assimilate pushed me into becoming an attention whore. I was only there for a limited engagement so I had to make an impression. Of course, other than a few college classes on childhood psychology, I am not overly qualified to make these assertions. You might have better luck slipping Lucy a nickel. For whatever the reason, I craved the spotlight. Like they say in Hollywood, there is no such thing as bad publicity.

From the onset these penguins...nuns had my number. I quickly learned they liked corporal punishment. Somehow, they had made it through their entire schooling without getting to the New Testament. I whole-heartily believe that had I slipped up and accidently threw a paper airplane with a needle taped to the front into the eye of another student...well they would have not hesitated to take one of mine.

I was paddled a lot...for silly infractions like: stomping in a mud puddle after I was told to *please avoid the mud puddle*, biting a girl's neck while playing a vampire at recess though I am not sure what they expected from a method actor such as myself, and breaking a girl's rib in defense of my friend of whom she had beaten badly the day before.

They had my number alright and it was apparent during our Christmas party. On Friday, toward the end of school, we were called to the cafeteria. Sister Mary Agnes, who was young and pretty and caused boys to have thoughts they shouldn't, was at the front surrounded by twenty five small, two-inch by three-inch boxes with red paper and one large one-foot square box with gold paper and a bow. She was by far my favorite, but I was so obnoxious just the day before I had made her cry. This hurt me.

Our eyes met for a moment...maybe I was mistaken, but the intense guilt I felt was no mistake. Yesterday changed me, but still I had lessons to learn.

"Children line up to select your..."

I leapt before she could say "presents." Before me lay an obstacle course of small creatures, classmates bent on capturing my prize. I took Taylor Van Pelt by the collar slowing him just enough to slip into that top spot, number one, head of the line. A few others laid in my destructive wake rubbing various ailing body parts. Normally, I would have had a great sense of accomplishment for my great feat, but as I looked up five nun-eyes were staring at me... it was weird Sister Marvin...well, her and two others. Sister Marvin wore a patch over one of her eyes. It didn't hamper her in any way as it was well documented she had another set in the back of her head.

Then the oddest thing happened, they smiled; all of them. I thought, *FOOL*, you let your guard down and now...! I envisioned them throwing their habits aside, not like smoking and drinking although those are habits, but not those habits, revealing Uzis spraying me full of... well... hate? They didn't move. They sat there with tight-lipped smiles as I slowly reached for and grabbed the *big* present. Only then did they stop looking at me and instead looked at each other, still smiling. Somehow, this triumphant victory had lost its triumphant *feel*.

Soon everyone was seated, boxes before them chatting, giggling, and enjoying. I sat alone, quiet, somber...enjoying? The nuns gave the *word* and kids tore into their boxes. I waited. I wanted to be the center of attention when I alone opened my gift. My classmates each held up identical, glistening, silver St. Christopher necklaces. I asked if I could hold one; heavy, solid, expensive. I coveted my neighbor's gift. Soon all eyes turned toward me. I slowly... methodically.... unwrapped the golden paper... lifted the lid.... there was a card on top; I tossed it to the side. The box, filled with shredded old missalettes seemed to be empty. As I dug my hands in, frantic my fingers sought something solid. Finally, bottom left corner; pay dirt.

I grabbed hold and pulled the item free from the opening. It took a few moments to realize what it was? A few beats and I had it. It was a man made from rolls of Lifesavers tied together with yarn; arms and leg two tubes each, body four tubes, hands, feet and neck each half tubes, for a total of fourteen and one half rolls. The head was poster board on a Popsicle stick with the face of Jesus. I didn't know how to react. A couple of kids snickered. I was embarrassed.

"Read the card, Brian," it was Sister Mary Agnes. I took the card and opened it. It was from her, Sister Mary Agnes.

Brian...

It had my name...the card that was sealed in the box beneath the golden paper already had my name...in Sister's handwriting.

Brian,

There are many lessons to learn in life. Each lesson, a gift from the one who taught it. My gift to you is not the candy doll, but rather who he represents. I made him for you; a gift from my own hands; a gift of love once given to me by a very old and wise penguin for a troubled, lost little girl. And a gift such as this is better than all others. He represents, the fact that no matter what you do, say, don't do, don't say...he always loves and forgives you; loved, even when you push people away, forgiven, even when you do things unforgivable. Always there, even when you think you need no one. Brian, we all need a Lifesaver every once in a while...you helped me remember.

Childhood moments such as these, form who we become as adults. I like to think I was fortunate enough to collect enough of these moments to alter the course of my personality. Even with loving parents and a solid family unit, I could have easily developed into a complete dickhead. And even though I am sure there are people in my life that would contend I still am a penisnoggin, I would argue, for the most part, the majority of people I have had contact with during the course of my adulthood would say I am not a phalicskull.

16

The Eighth Encounter

For the first time, I saw Mom the mouse while the sun was up. It was morning, just a couple of days after the surreal sleepover. I was in the kitchen frying up a couple of eggs for my wife. She likes them runny so she can dip her toast into the liquid, unfertilized chick fetus…I know they are not baby chickens, but I can't help but think that when I serve them. I have to have my yolk solid; eating a solid, chick fetus alleviates my concerns. The pans I use in the house are not of high quality. It is the frugal mentality I was brought up with that causes me to continually buy substandard products simply because of the price. I understand the reasoning of buying quality *once* versus crap five times, but I just can't bring myself to do it. If I have to buy a high ticket item at the store and need other things as well, I will make two trips to the store so I don't have to spend all the money at once. I know this is crazy, but it makes me feel less stressed.

Ironically, my mother always told me while I was growing up; I had champagne taste on a beer budget. Apparently, wanting a pair of Puma sneakers when K-Mart, Velcro strapped Traxx were available at a quarter of the price *and just as good*, made me into some sort of elitist. A little known fact about Puma was its creator was the brother of the creator of Adidas. The two Germans siblings, who probably dreamed of working together, thinking nothing could be better than to start a company with one's brother, got into a dispute, and now we have two separate brands of overpriced sneakers.

So, I am not sure where my frugality grew from as my mom clearly thought I was a spendthrift. Maybe the model my parents strictly adhered to subconsciously stuck with me as I matured. As a result, my frying pan's Teflon has long since been scraped away. I am sure it probably wasn't Teflon in the first place, but rather a thin layer of Teflon colored spray-paint applied by an eight-year old Malaysian child. So, my eggs stick; making soft-yolked creations a bit of a challenge. It just seems easier, to me, for my wife to change her eating habits…otherwise I am going to have to go out and buy a new pan when the one I have works perfectly fine; what a waste.

Like Adolf and Rudolf Dassler, the shoe brothers, my two brothers and I always talk about how cool it would be to teach in the same school. But, we all have big personalities and are very stubborn, so I am not so sure we wouldn't end up the same way. Maybe, it's just best we keep the fantasy alive. Sometimes reality disappoints.

I learned this one summer while chasing the girl in the black Trans-Am. Monte and Darrin were my buddies at the time and we first caught a glimpse of the car on Main Street. It went cruising by driven by a platinum blonde who looked to be a hot high-schooler. The stimulus of a giant firebird decal on the front of an awesome new sports car driven by a mysterious beauty triggered the inner-stalker in the three of us. We spent all down-time peddling our bikes around the town trying to find out where she lived. We must have seen her fifteen times or more during the course of the summer, but each time she was driving causing us to give chase yelling about *how hot she was* or *how cool the car looked*...always ending with *can we have a ride?* Toward the end of summer, it happened. Worn down by our persistence or just wanting to give three horny kids a thrill, she pulled over and told us to get in. OMG! Is what we would have texted had cell phones existed.

I was the biggest of us three and claimed the front seat as the other two slid in behind. The moment I got settled and looked at the driver my dream world collapsed. Seated to my left was an old woman of at least twenty-eight. Up close, her makeup was thick and too dark for her complexion. Her hair was a forced, unhealthy blonde and for the love of all that is sacred, she was wearing red-white-and blue Traxx tennis shoes. I'm not sure what we discussed, but what I do recall is an uncomfortable ride that lasted too long. It reminded me of the joke: There's only one thing that can make that woman look good...distance. It is the first time I remember thinking I wished I had just gone on with life not knowing the truth; it was better than reality.

Later, that year the same lesson was repeated in a different format. My friend, Darrin, lived on the other side of the tracks. And though that doesn't always mean what it implies, in this case it did. Darrin was a rough kid. Our house was just on the *right* side of the tracks directly across the street from a large electric power station. There was always a steady hum emanating in the air when we were out in the yard. If I had had sperm at that time in my life my children might have been born with flippers. The train still ran on the tracks that went down the center of the town. In the fall, a boy who was visiting and I didn't know, apparently was riding his mini-bike down the middle of the tracks and somehow crashed and got ran over by the train. My parents kept us sheltered as to the details, but the story became folklore at school.

Not to sound morbid, but a story such as this was pretty neat to kids who still thought hocking loogies for distance was good fun. At the time, as with many my age, I had been lucky to live an innocent life with no dramatic tragedies. So, there was a separation from the harsh reality of death and the intrigue of being so close to something so adult. Like the power lines, the story created a hum of its own. It was just fascinating that someone had died so close to my house. A kid doesn't think about parents crying over the loss of their child or funerals. We saw Wyle E. Coyote crushed to death time and time again every Saturday morning without any remorse or tears. The story wasn't real to us but something new and interesting to talk and laugh about.

This was true until Darrin and I were walking to his house one night. It was cold, but I don't remember any snow on the ground. As we tight-roped down the rails pretending if we fell off we would die as the gravel was molten lava, I saw it. I thought it was a weird caterpillar at first and bent to examine it further. It was not a bug at all but a finger; a real person's finger. I immediately called Darrin over to look and we poked it around with a stick for a bit. It didn't take us long to put two and two together and realize this was the finger of the mini-bike kid. We never bothered with his real name as it didn't enhance the story. The discovery of the finger, a boy's finger, brought to light what was hidden just a moment ago…the death at the railroad track was a kid, a real kid just like us. This tangible object changed our perception of the incident. At school when others tried to joke about what happened, we squelched it; the rough kid from the wrong side of the tracks and the new, big, fat kid.

The mouse caught me off guard. I was not sure if it was Mom or not. In fact, my first thought was to squash it. Old habits die hard. She came out of the pantry where the door was left open just a crack. She didn't make eye contact at all but was slinking about looking for cover in a manner very much like a regular mouse. I noticed the end of her black-tipped tail and knew it was Mom…but why the strange behavior?

It was during this brief moment of identification verification my wife decided to enter the kitchen to check on her eggs. She immediately saw the mouse and screamed. I wasn't prepared for any of this. Chaos! The truth of the matter was that seeing the mouse in the daytime acting in such a…well, natural way was confusing. Other than the black tip, I was feeling no sort of Mom-vibe. The high-pitched wail of my wife was not helping the clarity of my thoughts. She then started yelling, "Kill it, Brian! Kill it!" Okay, you can see my dilemma. On the *kill it* line, the mouse quickly ran back into the pantry.

I half-way listened to my wife pontificate about mice... how dirty they were...how they spread disease...how we need to get traps, but my thoughts were on the actions of my Mom...or mouse? Everything that had occurred up to this point was true, it happened; of this I was pretty certain. There were no dream sequences taking place. But, I would be lying if I didn't admit the mouse's behavior casted a rodent-sized shadow of doubt. At night everything just seemed more magical that for some reason cannot be recreated during daylight. It was the first time since the mouse and I's first meeting that reality got in the way of my fantasy and I was left confused and a bit angry it had happened. I interrupted my wife's diatribe with aggression. "You are over reacting as usual. I'll deal with it...as usual!" I was mad at her. No real reason, but she became the target of my frustration. It's like what they say about good business, "It's all about location, location, location."

One final side-note; the other day I was in K-Mart and saw they now sell Pumas.

17

Mouth Stretching, Brain Tumors and Butt Flexing

My children, along with my wife are a bit O.C.D.ey/ Tourettey acting. They aren't afraid to admit it. For example, my wife has this crazy, repetitive habit of annoying me every day; couldn't resist. My oldest son, when he was a baby used to roll his wrist in a repetitive motion. At first we thought something might be wrong. We lived in North Carolina and when we explained to the elderly, day-care lady we were concerned he might be autistic we were shocked by her response of, "Oh Honey, wouldn't that just be great?" After a brief pause she continued with, "He would be able to paint and draw."

My youngest is agitated when things are not a particular way he thinks they ought to be. He too has little quirks like eating all but a tiny bit of crust from sandwiches or pizza. I stood as a stalwart of normalcy as I discussed these issues with my mom. Her response was to remind me, I was a weird little bastard. She said, I may be *normal* now, though there was doubt, but she assured me this was not the case growing up. Apparently, my offspring didn't have a chance. These acorns not only didn't fall far from the tree; the tree was on an incline and they rolled right up to the trunk. Sorry guys.

As a kid I had three habits that were repetitive and distracting. Two were publically embarrassing to my mother and the other a bit hidden and confusing to her. The first behavior my poor mother had to deal with was the mouth stretch. I am not sure how it started, but once it did, I embraced it with the passion a horse fly takes in tormenting a sweaty, bald man's head in the summer. It felt so damn good. I would simply open my mouth as far as I could; making sure to stretch the thin flaps of skin on each side of my lips. This feeling was so gratifying I fear doing it today as I am afraid I could be sucked back into the vortex of ecstasy. I warn you as you read to not be lured into the siren song of the mouth stretch...you may never recover.

My mom thought I had gone nuts. This was back before the internet and Oprah, so she had no clue what was up with her kid. She flat out told me it was weird and if I kept it up, she wasn't going to take me out in public. I promised I would stop, but we both lied; I didn't stop and she still took me places. Mouth stretching was my meth. When winter rolled around and the air became dry, I developed seeping cracks on each side of my mouth. The slits would crust over, but with each new stretch, they were tore open once more. I continued to do this until I developed infantigo, a highly volatile bacterial infection that spreads. I soon had sores all over my face. I was a vain kid and still I couldn't stop. My mom, now not only had to deal with parading me around whilst I was looking like a baby bird in want of a worm, but she had the added shame of doing so with a scabby-faced, baby bird. As an adult you love your kids, but no matter who you are, you realize they are an extension of you when being judged by others. You shouldn't care what others think, but you can't help it.

Again, my mom had the added pressure of trying to make a good first impression to develop adult relationships...it's hard to fish for friends when your bait is a sore-laden adolescent who literally can't keep his mouth shut. I just stopped doing it one day. I don't recall the moment or what transpired to make me stop...I just did.

Mom survived this public shame only to later be introduced to the newest member of the family, Brian's random head shake. I was a bit older when I developed what I thought was a brain tumor. I could actually feel something hanging lose within my skull. As a result I felt the need to shake my head quickly from side to side as if trying to produce sound from a baby rattle. I would go a few minutes or so before I felt the need to do it, so I was able to hide it from people for a while. Plus, I had long bangs at the time so I would work in a hair-flip to mask the habit. Eventually, my mom noticed and wanted to know what was wrong with me...now? I told her she should sit down and brace herself. I then, as gently as I could, told her about my suspected brain tumor. She took it well, in fact she might have been smiling; a clear cover-up as to not show her inner pain. Here's the reality of the matter. I could have had a tumor. I could have. However, Mom did not take me to the doctor. In fact her response was, "It's all in your head." I know; that's where the tumor is.

One of three things could have caused her to not act. The first was she had her mom-sense turned to high and knew without a doubt I was fine and was just overreacting to another abnormal twitch. The second was she didn't *think* I had a tumor and figured with the cost of going to the doctor, it was worth the risk. And third, she knew I had a tumor and was hoping to get rid of me. I want to believe it was the first one, but in all fairness, knowing my family, I have to leave room it could have been the second.

My mom continued to take me with her when she went places. If she snuck out to the store every once in a while to avoid explaining what was wrong with her middle child and avoid the risk of me saying something along the lines of, "I have a brain tumor and no one will take me to the doctor," I wasn't the wiser and of course after having children of my own, wouldn't hold it against her if she did. Instead of Mom getting to run into people she knew and have them say parent flattering things like, "Look how tall Brian has grown," she faced the possibility of hearing something along the lines of, "I see Brian doesn't do that bizarre thing with his mouth now and only shakes his head in an off-putting movement that causes me to be uncomfortable around the both of you."

I shook my head for a couple more weeks, but my neck started to get sore and like a sunset…and the mouth stretch, the habit faded away. I did not die.

My last and secret habit was the buttocks flex. Much like the mouth stretch it felt really good. Again, I must warn you not to attempt this. Simply put, I would squeeze my butt muscles together and hold it for a second or two. It was a sensation that was pleasing, so I did it again…and again…and….I became addicted. This one went undetected for quite some time until I started to feel the need to do it while I was walking. At first, I would find reasons to stop so I could get in a solid, deep flex. It was something like, "Hold it a second. Was that Bobby across the street?" *full butt flex* "Never mind I was mistaken, let's keep going." But, then I advanced my skills to where I could do it without breaking stride. There was only a slight hiccup in my giddy up…*that* was what Mom noticed.

"Brian, why are you walking like you have a cob up your butt," was the way it was presented to me. I played dumb, replying I didn't know what she was talking about. When it happened again, I told her my underwear was in my crack. When it happened again, the gig was up or the jig, whichever you prefer. As embarrassing as it was, I came clean and told her exactly what I was doing. She reacted like she had caught me masturbating. I actually tried to convince her to try it. It was a dirty little exchange I wish I didn't remember. I felt like a drug pusher. "Come on just try it. You don't know what you're missing…come on, don't be afraid." If she did try it, which I am sure she did as no one can resist, just as you are going to as well, she never shared this fact with me. Her motherly advice, "Well, stop it! It's weird."

18

The Ninth Encounter

The very night following my wife's ordered mafia hit, my mom showed up again. At the time I really wasn't even thinking on the matter because my foot felt like someone had smashed it with a sledge hammer while I was sleeping. It was my fault as I performed the trifecta of no-no's. I had forgotten to take my pill that lowers my uric acid. I had a banner red-meat day with a hamburger lunch and a steak dinner, and I topped it all off with the final Gout forbidden taboo of beer...several.

Naked, I slunk out of bed, putting all of my weight on my good foot. There are various levels of pain and for a Gout sufferer you learn to have a very high tolerance. On a scale of 1 to 10, this was nearing a perfect score at 9.8. I always want to leave a little room so God doesn't come back with, "You think that's a 10? I'll show you a 10!" Needless to say, it hurt...a lot. I couldn't put any weight on it at all and for me to hop my over 220 pound body to the bathroom on one leg would have sounded like a hippo on a pogo stick. Not only would I have woken my wife, something I wanted to avoid, but I wasn't that confident in my good leg's ability to burden the whole load.

So, I went into this extravagant routine. We have hard wood floors throughout our house. I point this out because I have bad knees. I point this out because the two were about to meet.

My constantly sore knees are bi-products of many years of wrestling. I started the activity when I was just ten years old. It was actually a natural segue from my Judo days. I wrestled all through high school and then coached the sport for another twelve years. I spent more hours on all fours than a seasoned prostitute. The wear and tear just took its toll over time. Add into the mix one of my knees developed a disease, known as Osgood Schlatter when I was in Junior High and I was doomed to be the decrepit old man that rides his Hove-a-round scooter when visiting the Statue of Liberty. Named for the two doctors who discovered it, Robert Osgood and Carl Schlatter, the ailment usually occurs following a growth spurt...which was my case. So, along with basic puberty concerns of acne, dealing with the fact of not wanting to be the last boy in gym class to get pubic hair, a high-pitched voice crack when talking in front of girls, an elevated body odor, figuring out how to French kiss, finding good hiding places for the dirty magazines I found in a dumpster, learning the pattern so I could beat Pac Man, and deciding whether or not to grow out my hair long enough for a rat's tail, I had to deal with this as well.

Women always wonder why guys can be such pigs...they breed us this way in school. Where girls get separate stalls, boys learn to pee shoulder to shoulder. Sometimes a crude comment can help break the awkward tension. Most girl showers have partitions, but guys shower around a single pole...causing us to face each other. Whose idea was this? Hey, let's take pre-teen boys who are very self-conscious about their changing bodies and make them get naked and face each other so as they can make important comparisons such as body shape, penis size and who does and does not have inverted nipples. This in no way can be damaging. To handle these situations, we become desensitized to them and thus speak freely about topics that, to a woman, might be socially inappropriate. We *appear* to be crude pigs. Now you know.

Osgood Schlatters causes inflammation of a major tendon in the knee leading to excess bone growth which produces a visible lump just under the kneecap. It is very painful, especially when you hit that little sucker. Simple activities such as kneeling were rough. Not a good time to be Catholic where a mass work-out of stand-sit-kneel can seem like P90X. My knee became so bad at one point, that Mom said I didn't have to kneel. I tried it out one Sunday, but the disgusted look from the priest shamed me down. I just adjusted my weight to one side and leaned back so my butt was on the seat.

A brain tumor my mom didn't care about, but she took an interest in my knee. Maybe, because she could see the large swollen bump, making it real. Plus, I truly was in pain and like a good mom, she knew the difference. My parents decided I would not be allowed to play football my 8th grade year because of it. I was the starting quarterback the year before, so I this was a huge decision. Looking back I can't believe I let them get away with it. I really must have been in pain.

Getting down onto the hardwood floor on all fours was not something I wanted to do, but I had to get to the medicine cabinet and find some relief or it was going to be another long night. Zeke was awake, but didn't bother to get up just yet; checking to see what my next move was going to be. I lowered myself to the ground and pushed the dog off of the small pile of clothes I had worn the past few days. Zeke loved my smell. Maybe it just comforted him and made him feel closer to me. Our sense of smell is one of our strongest connections to memories. Every once in a while I will catch an odor in the air that immediately transports me back to the kitchen with Mom. If I could put those smells in a small pile, I would probably lie in them each night too.

I nudged the dog off the pile of clothes and found a couple of t-shirts. They were two I had bought a week after a Father's Day and Easter for just a few bucks; *Coolest Dad,* which is not true at all as it implies I am the coolest in the whole world and at best I am only the coolest in the Midwest region, and an Easter one with three baby chicks marching across the front with the words, *My Peeps.*

Growing up, Easter meant a new article of clothing, church and both a public and private egg hunt. The clothes were always some ugly pastel that would get worn just the once unless Mom could line up the annual family picture around the same time. Church was *the* Easter Catholic mass. The public hunt was the usual aggressive, push-n-pull at the local park that gave us a preview as to who was going to, years later, be shoved into school lockers and who was going to score both on and off the field. It was Easter after all and no mercy was to be given. We Weilerts, held our own.

The night before our *family* hunt we would always boil and color eggs. Mom set up the same holiday-type assembly line she did at Christmas. We would have all the colors using the small dye tablets mixed with vinegar, the eggs boiled and put back into their original cartons; a dozen for each child, dippers made out of wire coat hangers, Styrofoam cups with the bottoms cut out for drying and wax crayons that would leave the egg white were applied. It was this tool that allowed us to write Easter spirited sayings like, "Brad sucks eggs," on the actual egg. It was solid family time spent laughing and loving.

The next morning our treat on Easter was the satisfaction of finding those same eggs Mom and Dad cleverly hid and then later, eating those same eggs. No foo-foo, pansy chocolate or marshmallow or jelly beans; eggs, boiled eggs. When we found them all, we would hide them again and again until the sun got so hot in the late afternoon we figured we had better eat them before they got too bad; all twelve of those bastards. Our farts were horrible for days.

I wadded the t-shirts up to make them as thick as possible and slipped one under each knee. I then proceeded to slide my knees across the floor as I progressed on all fours. Zeke patiently walked behind me, just sniffing my butt once. My foot was absolutely killing me, but I caught a break as the cracking and popping pain in my knees gave me a much needed distraction. By the time I reached the kitchen, I was regretting my ill-conceived plan.

As I paused to catch my breath, and enjoy my discomfort, the rustling of papers drew my attention up to the bar. I peered up to see a mouse's head leaned over the edge peering down with eyes of concern. Sad eyes, as if she was empathizing with my suffering. I felt Zeke behind me as he licked the bottom of my foot as if saying, "I'm still here with you dude…I got your back." For the first time I became concerned Zeke might go crazy if he saw the mouse. Sure, he had been sleeping next to me during many of the mouse encounters with no reaction, and sure he was a dog and not a cat, and sure he was so old and disinterested in nearly all things there was no way he would put any effort out to eat the mouse unless she ran across his tongue, but I was not in a good frame of mind at the time and I panicked. I turned to face Zeke and growled to get him to back off into the bedroom. I was protecting my mom. At first he just stared at me like I had gone insane, which any other observer would have agreed with, but as I slid toward him he snarled a bit, but then thought better of it. Years ago, we already had this battle of who was top-dog during *the chicken incident*.

At the time we were living in the country and decided to buy some chickens so we could have fresh eggs every day. It went well for a while, but then they started to disappear.

We figured out Zeke had developed a taste. I was told by an old farmer to tape a dead chicken to the dog with duct tape behind his head until it rots. He swore, after that, the dog would never eat another chicken. So, I tried it. I took one of the dead chickens I found in the yard and taped it to his head.

Weeks went by and Zeke and his hitchhiker friend stunk so bad you couldn't stand to be fifty feet from them. I finally decided he had learned his lesson and went to take the chicken off. It was then he and I had an awful, aggressive interaction. As I grabbed his collar, he turned to bite me. He was growling and jerking about, trying to tear into me. My death grip on the collar was all that was keeping me alive. My knuckles were caked in blood from decaying chicken and a few glancing teeth marks. All the noise drew my kids into the yard and they were instantly terrified by the scene. There was their dad locked in a bloody battle with a wild beast. They were screaming, "Stop it!" and crying. With my free hand I balled up my fist and socked Zeke hard in the head. He stopped struggling and lay down. My kids were still screaming, but now I realized I had the situation all wrong. They were telling me to *stop it*. "Dad, you're hurting him!"

Zeke and I are dearest of friends, but from that point on, we both knew who was in charge. But, the story doesn't end there. We were now down to just one chicken and I vowed to keep it alive. For weeks we all lived in harmony and I felt the duct tape, chicken fiasco may have all been worth it.

Until one evening when I returned from wrestling practice and went to put the chicken up for the night and couldn't find her. When I located Zeke on the back porch, we made eye contact and I could just tell he was guilty. Dogs are horrible liars. He made a mistake of glancing away and staring at a spot in the yard. My eyes followed his gaze to what appeared to be two chicken legs sticking out of the ground. I quickly moved in that direction and pulled the poultry carrot from the dirt. The skin of her breast was split open, but miraculously, the hen was still alive. Apparently, Zeke had started to eat her and then realized the folly of his ways and tried to hide the evidence. I had heard Blue Heelers were smart, but this animal's behavior was too human.

I took the hen inside and my wife sewed up her chest. We kept her in a box with a heat lamp through the night. We thought there was no way she could survive...but not only did she survive, in the morning she had laid an egg. When she had fully healed and was released back into the yard, she and Zeke actually became friends. It was nothing to come home and see the two of them lounging in the sun on the sidewalk.

I growled one more time and Zeke turned and went back to the bedroom. I don't know if it was because he was intimidated or because he was too old to care about pissing matches. I spun back around to see if Mom was still there, she was.

Using a stool for support, I pulled myself up to my foot. I reached out to touch Mom, and she let me. I very softly stroked her head with my index finger; she was fragile. I turned my hand palm up and she crawled into it.

I no longer am going to make excuses for what I write. Either you believe or you don't. I will make no more efforts to convince those who would call me nuts. Quite honestly, it doesn't matter. I am convinced all that happened to me was solely for me anyway. Simply sharing the story with others is something I felt my mom would have liked. She always enjoyed reading my stories.

I held her in my hand for a moment and then suddenly felt as Adam might have in the Garden of Eden; I was naked in front of my mom. Though she would have told me, "You've seen one, you've seen 'em all," I still felt awkward. So, I did something I used to do with my gerbil; I put her on my head. I hoped that unlike Cuthbert, Mom would choose not to use my hair as a latrine.

As much as this moment was what some would call magical, it really felt somewhat normal. My foot was still causing agonizing pain and I couldn't concentrate on anything. I dropped back to all fours and made my way to the bathroom medicine cabinet. It's times like this where the saying, "I wish I had a camera," really applies; the heroic, cowgirl mouse atop her chubby nude, hobbled steed...all that was missing was squeaked, *Giddy up!* What a sight.

In the bathroom I once again stood, being careful not to disturb Mom. Moving like I had a book atop my head whilst reciting, *the rain in Spain falls mainly on the plain.* I peered in the mirror to see what a mouse on my head looked like. It was every bit as cool as I could have imagined. Her little hands were gripping two separate strands of hair like makeshift reigns. Her head was up and she too was scoping out the mirror to see what a head below her looked like. It must have been every bit as cool for her as her eyes seemed alive and amused. It was fun and funny. I laughed out loud. I am sure if mice could laugh, Mom would have joined in.

I took a couple of anti-inflammatories and a few pain pills and proceeded to the freezer for an ice-pack. My knees had enough punishment so I used whatever I could as a crutch...the door jamb to the back of couch...*one hop*, I could feel Mom's body rise and fall on my head...to the bar to the freezer and back to the bar...*one hop*...back to the couch and sit. I was breathing heavy from the workout. I propped my foot up, put the icepack in place and waited for the medicine to kick in. This was my life for far too many evenings. I wasn't sure how to get Mom out of my hair which is something I am sure she figuratively struggled with concerning me. I guess turnabout is fair play. I sat there waiting for her to make a move. She didn't. I felt the slight pressure from her feet as she turned a few circles and then entirety of her body as she lay down.

This moment was so peaceful. I sat in silence smiling. I couldn't help it. The pain went away far sooner than it normally did; in fact I had forgotten about it all together. I closed my eyes and slept.

19

Cuttin' Cane and Water Witching

My cell phone died the other day, just like watches or anything else with a battery that comes into contact with my body for any length of time. It is a family trait passed down from my father's side. I think the high uric acid is involved in some manner. Though it sounds bizarre, the reality of it all is we are each just big electric power plants. Here is some empirical proof of my condition. I no longer can wear a watch as they all stop working within a month or two. My mom did try to get clever and buy me a watch band that went under the actual watch. This had only slightly better results as the watch made it nearly half the year. Once in the Coast Guard while on a risky rescue in a large storm, every time I touched the radio to communicate back to the boat it *zapped* out. I had to have someone else hold the mic while I talked. At a football game while working security, I had a spare nine-volt battery in my pocket for the walkie-talkie. The battery became so hot it burned my leg. You could not hold it in your hand. If I could learn to harness these powers, I just might become a super hero.

The final manifestation of the electric abnormality is that most of my family has the ability to water witch. I know this skill has many nonbelievers, but I can't help their ignorance. I am able to take two bent wires, I use cut up coat hangers, place them loosely in each hand and when I pass over a water source, the two wires cross. It looks like a parlor trick and the first time I saw my dad do it to locate a well, I thought he was full of it. But, as I saw him do it again and again over the years and I myself tried it with success…I came to realize this was just one more super power I possessed. "Stand back villain or I will kill your expensive cell phone thus causing you to lose all your contacts. I'm warning you, if you dare take one more step I will also inform you if you are standing over a water source."

If alive during the time the west was being settled and wells were an important part of being able to survive, I'm sure I would have been in high demand and been able to name my price. But, alas, I do not live during that time. The only real effect of this electrical charged power is, I have to continually pay money for things that should last longer. Cell phones are not cheap.

At an early age we were taught the value of money and hard work. My dad still is one of the hardest working men I know and he's retired. As a sixth grader, I was introduced to my first summer job. I guess Mom got used to having us out of the house during the school year and figured if she could keep us busy she could not only have continuous peace and quiet, but also keep us out of trouble. Mom arranged for us to work for a local farmer cutting weeds from the fields of his various crops. This was before genetically-modified, weed- resistant seeds and other advancements.

During this era, it was cheaper for a farmer to give a couple of twelve year olds giant machetes, called corn knives, and let them do what twelve year old boys to naturally; destroy things. Mom would pack me a lunch and fill a small cooler with ice and water and then my dad would drop us off at the farm before light and then head off to work. The job was mentally simple but physically hard. From sunup until late afternoon, we would walk the rows of corn, soybean, or milo and whack any weed we saw to the ground. At first this was really fun, but fun quickly turned to monotony. Every once in a while we would catch a brief entertainment break by coming across giant garden spiders sitting in the center of their webs which were stretched across our walking paths. We would turn the blades to the flat edge and pretend we were taking batting practice. The pay was next to nothing, but it gave us enough spending cash to get some candy, go to the bowling alley and play pinball and Pac Man. Working made us feel like men. We no longer needed to ask our mommies for money. We were growing up.

20

The Tenth Encounter

Midway through the night, I suddenly woke to an almost undetectable scratching noise. It took me a second to orient myself, but I soon realized I was still on the couch. A beat later and I remembered Mom on my head. I slowly reached up to locate her. She wasn't there. The scratching noise came once again from the kitchen. I got up. If it weren't for the icepack falling to the floor I wouldn't have remembered having a gout attack at all. My foot felt fine. The scratching was coming from the pantry.

Before I could open the pantry door, I caught something out of the corner of my eye toward the back porch. I turned to see Leon, staring at me through the window. This cat was a warrior; a giant, uncut tom who would nightly patrol the neighborhood in search of pussy. Several times he returned in the morning with his face torn from battle. I am sure if he could speak, he would say, "You should see the other guy." Leon seemed very interested in what I was doing...too interested. I made a hissing noise and waved my hands to try and get him to leave. He just licked his lips and held his ground. He was a mean bastard who wouldn't let you even pet him. He wasn't afraid of me. I walked over and pulled the curtain shut. He didn't move.

Back at the pantry, I fully opened the door, pulled the chain to turn on the light and peeked inside. The sound was coming from behind a pile of discarded *momentary must-have* appliances that were supposed to ease the drudgery of cooking...but were so seldom used as to not warrant permanent counter space. Plus, they really were too time consuming to set up and clean to ever see the light of day past their maiden voyages. Joined together in a shabbily constructed stack were: A George Forman grill, a Crockpot that in fairness did get used on occasion, a dehydrator, a cake decorating kit, a Fry Daddy, an awesome blossom onion cutting contraption, a ravioli press, and several Tupperware containers that had misplaced lids. Add to the mix an assortment of paint cans which we know matched colors in the house but for the life of us couldn't remember which rooms, enough cleaning supplies to make a hoarder's house sparkle, brooms, mops, plastic picnic ware, an old shotgun we found in the attic that looks like it came from a stage coach and we always said we should get appraised, extra paper towels and toilet paper, and I was looking at Wal-Mart's version of the Berlin Wall.

It was from behind this mass the muffled scratching was emanating. I began the task of quietly moving items to get to the source. Finally, after several minutes I saw her. It was Mom and she was in the far corner frantically moving her fingernails on a box of Biz. How old was that? We didn't even use Biz anymore. When she saw me she immediately stopped. I instantly knew she wanted me to find her.

Once in a grocery store I was distracted in the cereal aisle by the array of colored, cartooned boxes and the promise of hidden prizes in their bottoms. When my curiosity had run its course and I turned to continue shopping with my mom, I followed a pair of legs for a couple of minutes never bothering to look up. When I did, I realized the legs did not belong to Mom, but a large woman impersonator. I don't know how old I was, of course, but I was young enough to be afraid; as if I were all of a sudden thrown in the middle of a hostile world with little hope of return. Not being a shy child, I began to scream, "Mom!" I know this happens to most kids at least once during their life, but the sudden sense of the loss of your mother really hits you hard. It was the first reality check of how devastating it would be to not have her in my life. When I found her I clung so tightly I almost knocked her over. I was crying, "I thought I had lost you." She just rubbed my head and told me, "It's okay, I am right here. I would never leave you, silly."

Next to the box of Biz, Mom stood in what can only be described as a large nest. The nest was comprised of a fluffy pile of chewed paper. I could see the paper had writing on it so I reached in and pinched a small sample. On one slip, I was able to make out the words, *my panties off and throws them on the floor*...I recognized them. I had bought a copy of *50 Shades of Grey* after a person told me they thought I would be able to get a forensics cutting from it for competition. They assured me it wasn't *all* filthy. I secretly read it and hid it away in the pantry. I'm not sure why. I guess I didn't want my wife to know I was reading it, but more likely, I didn't want my wife to read it and have expectations from me I wasn't capable of living up to. Now here it was.

My mom and dad were both super talented and smart, but as with many who grew up during that era, they opted to get married and start a family. My father had been a stud linebacker in high school and had a football scholarship to play at Pittsburg University; the small one in Kansas. Had he gone, during his four years he would have been a member of a national championship team and a classmate of Gary Busey, who dropped out just one credit shy of a degree. But, he chose to get training in a job that allowed him to use his hands...he had talent there as well. My mother was a veracious reader; a habit that made her an excellent student. However, these high school sweethearts' lives took them down a different path. My mom continued to read, but her passion turned to what we called, trashy romance novels with covers adorned with shirtless men with long flowing hair. I know looking back it was an escape for a woman trapped in a house with three kids. In her reality, there were never exotic romantic trips to Europe. Her and my father's love was a foundation built from a different material. A strong foundation based on need, trust and family. Though they told each other they loved each other often, theirs was a love that didn't require it. My mom could read a book a day if given the time. She consumed them. It was her dirty little secret.

Seeing a nest of the shredded remains of what some coined *mommy porn* surrounding my mom caused me a bit of embarrassment. I whispered the lie, "I didn't buy it...or read it." But, I was also thinking, that this was just the kind of book Mom would have read at night after we children went to bed. Tucked down in were other seemingly random items. But, as I examined them, I realized...not random, but deliberate. There as a penny from 1966, the year I was born. My hands were shaking as I reached down and picked up a keychain with a miniature school bus attached.

Mom decided it was time for her to go to work. We had finally settled down in Wamego and her children were gone at school and involved in every sport. She landed a job as a bus driver. Interesting enough we weren't allowed to ride the bus. At this time, schools didn't bus kids that lived within the city limits. Our house was in a newly annexed subdivision that was across a highway opposite the town. Our house was on the last street of that subdivision so, our morning walk to school was not only a mile and a half in distance, but also required us to cross the highway.

One of my mom's claims to fame was her fight to get a stop light put up at that crossing. You would have thought she was asking them to erect a statue of Hitler. Our town only had one other stoplight at the time, so suggesting a whole other one must have appeared to be *just crazy talk*. Plus, why on Earth would they stop the major thoroughfare for a bunch of school children? Again you have to love the mentality of *there hasn't been one killed yet* of the 1970's. But, one thing they didn't know, was what this woman had dealt with during the course of her life. They were outmatched, they just didn't know it. I am sure the reasoning was, to tell this housewife *no* and she would disappear. She didn't. My mom had set her mind on the fact, this was necessary for the safety of her kids…she had put in the hard labor of raising us this far and didn't want to leave it up to the Darwinian fate of a semi-truck. I am not sure exactly when the paradigm shifted from, *I hope you kids don't do anything so stupid you die*; to, *I better do something to prevent these kids from doing something so stupid they die…*but the switch was made. Today, if you drive through Wamego along Highway 24, be prepared to stop at the intersection of Lilac Lane.

My mom loved driving the bus. Many troubled kids were drawn to her tough-love, no-bullshit approach to life. She had raised the likes of me and no one was going to throw her off her game now. I had unwittingly prepared her for battle. As my own children were born and grew to know their grandmothers, they separated and named them by the most iconic symbols associated with each woman. My wife's mom, Anna, became Grandma Clown, and my mom became Grandma Bus. As a bus driver, she was able to drive to all the *away* sporting events in which we were involved. This allowed her, not only to travel free of cost, but avoid the huge gas price of nearly a dollar a gallon. So, she got paid to watch us compete. She was a frugal Weilert through and through.

I had taken the keychain from her dresser after the funeral. It was a small keepsake with which my children connected. This whole mouse thing had turned me into a softy. I was crying again. I hated doing it. Emotions were an unwelcomed foreigner glancing behind the manly, stoic façade I had carefully crafted over these many years.
The final item was something I didn't recognize at first. I picked it up and turned it over a few times. I knew my mom wanted me to find all of this to remove any doubt of

what I was experiencing. She didn't know I had bought
what she was selling long ago. Then, I had it. It had been
four years; I knew the mouse couldn't have been alive. We
had sealed it below the earth, but even if we hadn't...even
if I had somehow unthinkingly put it in my pocket....my
wife, after hundreds upon hundreds of loads of laundry
would have found it. So, there was no way it could be
here...but here it was. In my hand I held a small, broken-
off chunk of stained and varnished wood.

After I gave my mother's vault a good two coats of
molasses and had faced my public ridicule from the family,
I moved to a second task of creating an urn to hold Mom's
ashes. The cheap plastic container from the crematory was
functional and would have been fine, but I needed a project
to occupy my mind. I constructed it out of wood and made
it to where the plastic container would slip inside, out of
site. When you are grieving not all of what you remember
is clear. I think I did this project alone, but could have had
some help from my brothers. I include this so as to not hurt
their feelings if this is indeed true. The urn came together
as if my hands were being guided. It was a tall container
with a rosary I made from large wooden beads wrapped
around leading to a large cross that sat atop the lid. It was
stained and varnished. I was so proud.

At the funeral we eventually came to a point where the urn
was lowered into the vault. Many people had told me how
beautiful it was. Somehow, while putting it in place and
trying to lower the lid of the vault, my poor cousin broke a
corner off the cross. He felt so horrible; I could
immediately see it on his face... you would have thought
he killed her. I let him have it with the truth. I, who had
literally sugar-coated things from the start, thought it was

time for some brutal honesty. I told him not to worry. I told him it was funny. As morbid as that sounds it was. I smiled to myself. My mom would have thought it was funny. Hell, it was funny...the poor bastard.

It was this corner of the cross I held in my hand. My mom knew I had figured it out. Though a myriad of tears I stared at this small four-legged miracle hunkered down in the corner of my pantry...her eyes were smiling. A moment later, as if satisfied, she crawled to the center of the nest, turned a few circles and lay down to sleep. I watched for a just a bit longer, "Goodnight. I'll see you soon....love you."

21

Terriers, a Greased Pig and the Tree

It is odd the only dog I ever owned is a scary beast...to everyone but me; odd, because I have a fear of dogs. My wife has learned this over the years and sort of thinks it's funny, "Oh, big tough guy afraid of a wiener dog." I should point out; I have never met a nice one. My wife and I always hold hands when we walk. When we approach a yard with a barking dog, whether on a chain or not, my wife will switch sides with me so she will be the first to be eaten. She really isn't that brave, she's like a canine version of Jane Goodal. Even if it were a rabid pit-bull from Michael Vick's yard, she would have it licking her hand and pounding the ground with its hind leg as she finds that perfect spot to scratch right behind the ear. Deep down I know I could easily crush the neck of most small dogs beneath my feet if attacked, but this all stems from those damn Scottish terrier twins.

It was kindergarten or first grade and on the inaugural day Mom took me to the new school to make sure I didn't freak out or do something to alienate myself, kissed me and was gone. On day two she informed me I could walk to school with a neighbor kid. We were just two blocks from school. I was excited to have that level of trust and appreciated her confidence in me. I met up with the boy and headed to school; one block down and one to go. It was then it happened. Two black Scottish terrors, and yes *terrors* is the exact word, came out from a yard and went ape-shit on me. They never made physical contact, but they were barking and, yes terrorizing me. My classmate and I went into a full sprint and after a brief chase the terrors gave up and returned to their yard. I was shaken. It was so sudden. One moment we were talking about why Aquaman seemed like the weakest link of the Justice League and the next we were involved in a vicious ambush. It shook my belief in the safety of being alone outdoors, something that had never crossed my mind.

The third day my neighbor boy didn't show and I was faced with the choice of telling my mom, I couldn't go to school alone or surrender my independence. It was a difficult choice; like an adolescent version of the Patriot Act. I had to decide just how much freedom I was willing to give up to feel safe. Unlike congress, I opted for freedom. I never told my mom a thing. I never saw the neighbor again and can only assume he opted for safety and his mother was driving him to school. From that day on I walked four blocks to school, navigating a square around the twin hazards. I never forgot the fear I felt that day, but I also didn't surrender. I pressed on. I know Mom would have been proud...well, until she knew the reason.

She learned to not only adjust to my independent nature, but respect it. Sometimes she even used it.

We moved to Wamego around the 4th of July. One of the festivities was a grease pig competition. If you haven't seen one, they are not complicated. A small pig is lathered up with some slick substance and released in a pen with no less than fifteen crazed children trying to grab hold and carry the frightened creature to a predetermined circle spray-painted in the dirt. As you can probably tell, this is not an activity you would find at PETA's annual family picnic. We were not going to participate. Being new to the area we were going to sit back and get the lay of land by watching and listening to kids and parents. As if we were aliens visiting Earth, we had become experts over the past years on how to temper our initial contact so as to fit in. We were doing just that when some sort of verbal altercation occurred between my mother and some other mother. To be honest, I have a feeling this nearly forty year old memory wouldn't stand up to cross examination. But, I can only go with how I remember it going down. The issue must have been along the classic *my _____ is better/bigger than your _____* vein, because the next thing I know, Mom is telling me I am now entered into the grease pig event. Apparently, some rules go out the window when family pride is on the line as I was allowed to enter the pen wearing one of my *good* t-shirts. Though this was supposed to be a fun time, I felt as a gladiator might when he stepped into the arena for a fight to the death. I was a bit tubby, but I was a very athletic tubby. I think I was underestimated by the crowd. I would have gone off in Vegas as an 82-1 long shot. The whistle blew and everyone gave chase. My mom didn't say anything, but I knew it was important to her for me to win. I didn't disappoint. After it was over and I returned to the stands, Mom was all smiles. Whoever she was fighting with and whatever they were fighting about had evaporated when I stood in that circle with a squealing, future pork chop.

Mom didn't always like to watch us compete. During wrestling season, she would drive the bus so she could watch us only to get up from the bleachers and hide in the hallway before our matches. She would peek around the corner from time to time to check on the score. This was not a one year thing. If you took the start and finish of the total number of years my brothers and I competed you would find she did this routine from 1976 until 1988. She loved the sport, but watching her babies put in a position to where they could get hurt was too much; so much of her life had been dedicated to just us. I really think the *hurt* she feared was not physical, but emotional. She had to be our protector so often, as we moved from place to place trying desperately to help us fit in; she couldn't give up that role. It's not like we were bad either. All three of us are in the Wamego high school Hall of Fame for our wrestling.

Wrestling was an unpoliced sport during those years in regard to weigh loss. As a result, kids would do ridiculous things to make it to a lower weight class: starving for days, eating Ex-lax like chocolate, purging, wearing plastic bags under sweats while jump roping in the lockerroom with all the showers turned on full blast hot to create a super sauna, chewing tobacco so you could spit, popping diuretics, and using leaches. Okay, the leaches were a fabrication, but only because I didn't think of it back then. I once did have a teammate who punched himself in the nose to bleed out a bit so as to make weight.

Not only did the state not have any guidelines, apparently coaches and even my own parents were unaware of what we were doing, or just didn't care. To put the insanity in perspective, at the beginning of my fifth grade year I weighed 115 pounds. Four years later, my freshman year of high school, I wrestled varsity at 98 pounds. I was so emaciated; the team called me the politically incorrect Auswitch Jew. Mom noticed the changes, but never said a word. She kept right on making sugar-free Knox Blox, a wrestling family favorite. All three of us boys were good at it and because of this; I think mom turned a blind eye. I am sure it felt good to her to have us be popular and hear positive comments from other adults. With the stability of home, she was finally getting to reap some of the benefits from the years of hard labor. She deserved it.

But, as we grew older, we needed her less and less. After we all moved on, except my sister, Mom transitioned from bus driving to work as a secretary at the middle school. It is at this middle school she impacted so many young lives. She worked there until she retired; the year of her death. This impacts me every day in my decisions. I don't want to work at a job that feels like a job. I want to inspire and be inspired. I think my mom loved what she did. Her whole life had been dedicated to her own children, that in the end, being a mother was what she knew; it was what she was good at. At the school, they planted a tree in her honor upon her passing. Though I have not been to her grave, I have been to the tree. It seems easier to look at a living thing.

22

The Final Encounter

Something wasn't right when I woke in the morning. I couldn't place what it was...but something. My wife was still asleep as I rose to make some coffee. I went about the well-practiced routine when she yelled from the bedroom.

"Brian, will you check the trap?"

Even though I heard her, I ran the familiar spousal, double-check script, "What?"

"The trap...I bought some of those sticky traps at Wal-Mart to get rid of the mouse you said you would *deal with*."

Silence

"Will you check it?"

Silence

"Brian, do you hear me?"

"Yeah."

"It's in the pantry…okay?"

"I said, yeah."

I walked over to the door. It was open just a sliver, a sliver the size a mouse could squeeze herself through. I paused. I knew. As I pulled the knob, I saw her stuck to this large yellow square. Her entire left side was pressed hard against the surface rendering her immobile.

"Did we get it?" My wife called from the bedroom.

I quickly responded, "No, empty." I tried so hard to remain calm, but I was panicked and angry. I think it is fair to say I hated my wife at that moment. I told her *I* would take care of it. How dare her!

"Leave it there. I bet we get it tonight." She sounded so damn peppy.

I looked back down at Mom and she was still breathing, but it was a mess. Her struggles during the night had made things worse. My head was swirling. I was on the verge of tears as I picked up the trap, trying to keep it level.

"I need to run out to the garage and get something." I lied to my wife who I knew wouldn't let it go without questioning.

"What do you need in the garage at this time in the morning?"

I thought quickly, "I think we have some real mouse traps out there. I want to set some of those."

"Oh, okay. Try to be quiet though, I want to sleep a bit more…okay?"

I was already moving out the door toward the garage. I wasn't sure why I went there. Maybe it is just an innate guy thing to head that direction when something needed to be fixed. I walked carefully as if a butterfly had landed on my palm and I was trying to make my way across the yard to show Mom before it flew away; soft and fast.

I sat her down on the workbench. I was crying. "Mom, what have you done? Look at you." I leaned down and stared into her one eye. She couldn't move at all. I could see the rapid, steady beat of her heart. I put my finger onto the surface of the trap in one of the corners to try and determine just what I was dealing with. I thought if it wasn't too sticky, I could in some way peel her off and clean her up and everything would be okay. My finger stuck. I struggled to get it off without getting my other hand stuck like some Three Stooges episode where glue is involved.

I tried to pry up Mom's tail with a screw driver so as to have something to pull, but it just wasn't going to happen. The screw driver got stuck. I don't know who makes these traps, but if it was larger, it could keep a human captive.

I tried everything, but there was no way to get her off of it without pulling her tiny body apart.

At some point I stopped. I had faced this before. How do you say goodbye to your mother?

I leaned down once more and kissed her on the head. My tears fell onto the trap where they were repelled.

The soul of a person can be seen inside the eye. I believe this. I was looking at my mom. God, I knew it. She was there and no one will ever be able to make me think otherwise. You can call my crazy all you want, but I know what happened.

I knew what I had to do. Something I owed her four years ago.

"Mom, I'm so sorry I didn't say goodbye. My God, how I love you. You will always be with me. *Always.* I can only hope to be a man who will always make you proud. I will pray for you and hope you will do the same for me as I muddle my way through this life. I'll help keep tabs on Dad and make sure he doesn't starve. I know you worried about that. I guess you were right, you truly are now, *in the hands of God* and I pray I will see you again. Goodbye Mom, I love you."

Maybe, Mom knew all along I had to clear this before I could move forward. Maybe that is why she came back into my life. She blinked a couple of times and a small tear formed at the corner of her eye. I know people will say this is too much, my little fable has gone too far… but, I don't care. I really don't. The truth is the truth.

A few seconds later, Mom was gone. The mouse was still breathing, but the beady little eye was dark. Like Elvis, Mom had left the building. But, before she left, she gathered the large burden of guilt I had carried these past four years and all the anger I had for my wife and took them with her. In a way, without my wife I would never have been able to do what I had to do. Mom couldn't stay as a mouse forever; a wild rodent's life expectancy is less than a year. I realized it was part of a bigger plan. This was supposed to happen.

I guess no one really knows what happens when we die, but I know it is not the end. We do have a spirit that lives on; separate from the carcass we are forced to drag through life. I know there are skeptics, but I choose to believe my mom's soul floated to heaven that morning. She was an awesome woman and I will miss her every day I walk this planet. But, in the end, if I can get my shit together...maybe we can see each other again. Wouldn't that be awesome?

I respectfully pushed down on the mouse's frail body with a rag to put her out of her misery. It was the least I could do for her. I then wrapped the trap completely around her, walked to the garbage cans in back of the garage and tossed her in.

My Dad used to always say that if you reached your hand into a bucket of water and then pulled it out, the hole it would leave is how much the world would miss you when you were gone...he was wrong.

The End

ABOUT THE AUTHOR

Along with writing, Brian Weilert is a debate/speech coach in Kansas. He has been happily married for over twenty-five years to his wife, Stacia, and has two grown sons, Levi and Baker. He has been professionally writing for the past fourteen years. His short stories, poems and scripts have successfully been used for speech competitions at all levels.